# THE CONVERSION

BOOKS BY AHARON APPELFELD

*Badenheim 1939*

*The Age of Wonders*

*Tzili: The Story of a Life*

*The Retreat*

*To the Land of the Cattails*

*The Immortal Bartfuss*

*For Every Sin*

*The Healer*

*Katerina*

*Unto the Soul*

*Beyond Despair:*
*Three Lectures and a Conversation with Philip Roth*

*The Iron Tracks*

# THE
# CONVERSION

*Aharon Appelfeld*

TRANSLATED FROM THE HEBREW
BY JEFFREY M. GREEN

*Schocken Books, New York*

All rights reserved under International and Pan-American Copyright
Conventions. Published in the United States by Schocken Books
Inc., New York, and simultaneously in Canada by Random House of
Canada Limited, Toronto. Distributed by Pantheon Books, a division
of Random House, Inc., New York. Originally published in Israel as
*Timyon* by Keter Publishing House Ltd., Jerusalem, in 1991. Copyright
© 1993 by Aharon Appelfeld and Keter Publishing House Ltd.

SCHOCKEN and colophon are trademarks of Schocken Books Inc.

Library of Congress Cataloging-in-Publication Data

Appelfeld, Aharon.
[Timyon. English]
The conversion / Aharon Appelfeld ; translated from
the Hebrew by Jeffrey M. Green.
p.   cm.
ISBN 0-8052-4153-1
I.  Green, Yaacov Jeffrey.   II.  Title.
PJ5054.A755T5613   1998
892.4'36—dc21                                    98-18169
CIP

Random House Web Address:
http://www.randomhouse.com/

Book design by Suvi Asch

Printed in the United States of America
First Edition
2   4   6   8   9   7   5   3   1

# THE CONVERSION

## C H A P T E R

### I

The ceremony was short, subdued, and without ostentation. Only afterward, in the church's reception room, did the voices return to normal. Wine, homemade pastries, and sweets were served. Schmidt, the lawyer, hugged Karl warmly, as if a business deal and not a solemn ceremony had at last been concluded. The touch of the lawyer's hand once again brought school before Karl's eyes, the graduation parties and his Aunt Franzi's bright face, an entire life that now flowed into the abyss with a deafening roar.

Karl checked his emotions and shook the guests' hands with a smile. The more faces that passed before him, the clearer it became: there was no going back.

He had known most of them as classmates. Now in their thirties, some of the men were bald, and the women had become grim little housewives. Only yesterday these faces had been open and alive. Now the years had sealed them up. For a moment he forgot the ceremony, and the memories that passed filled him with gloom. That lasted only a moment. The hands that were extended to him from all sides were familiar. A few secret enemies, perhaps, but he knew that if he were ever in trouble he could depend on most of them.

Several guests surrounded Father Merser and congratulated him too. Father Merser seemed to tower above everyone, perhaps because he was still wearing his long priestly garb. His sister, Miss Clara, gaily offered cream puffs. Everyone knew her too. She was a pretty woman, around forty. She had been the cause of a few scandals that had been resolved with her brother's help. Father Merser was fond of her and would bring her to ceremonies like this one, to demonstrate that she had reformed.

On the other side of the room cognac and liqueurs were being served. A tall man stood in the center, Slavic-sounding words rolling off his tongue. With his long arms he made some elaborate gesture, and everyone around him erupted in laughter. Karl remembered him too, but couldn't recall his name.

The spell of the ceremony gradually faded, and everyone grew hungry. A ceremony like this is no more than a tonsillectomy, one of his childhood friends had told him. But Karl now felt differently: as if his legs were weighed down.

In the corner stood a woman, not young, dressed in old-fashioned clothes. It was Aunt Franzi's friend. She too had dreamt of a career in the theater. She had studied in Russia, with Stanislavsky, for several years. Upon her return she had married an impoverished nobleman and settled on the outskirts of town. Aunt Franzi was very close to her and would describe her as "a great woman who was crushed by the provinces like a fly." Karl crossed the room and hugged her gently.

"We all end up here," she said with a good-natured smile.

"So it seems."

"I did it while my parents were living, and I regret it to this day. Things like this should be done secretly, under the cover of night, don't you think?"

"How did you hear about it?"

"The church bells, my friend, didn't they ring? I don't live far from here. I see and hear everything."

"Lovely."

"How is Aunt Franzi?"

"I haven't seen her in years."

"We're criminals," she leaned over and whispered. "Those who are dearest to us we neglect. In the world to come, they'll whip us like dogs."

Father Merser circulated among the guests, most of

whom he knew well. He had even married some of them. Though pleasant enough, he was not well liked. "No one easily forgets the one who converts him," Karl's friend Erwin had once said in a moment of insight.

Afterward, Karl spoke passionately of the need to institute certain municipal laws to decrease friction between citizens and the authorities. His words didn't suit the event. They sounded as if written for a different audience, but no one objected. Everyone was caught up in the celebration, which rushed along with a gay murmur.

Martin Schmidt, the lawyer, approached Karl again. "Everything went very nicely."

"It was simpler than I had imagined it."

"Father Merser is a very pleasant man."

"True."

"And very tactful," added Martin.

"So it seems."

Martin Schmidt had converted more than ten years before, with his parents' permission, and since then he had attended every conversion in the city. This time there was an additional reason: he and Karl had been close friends since childhood. Martin's early conversion had put a crimp in that long friendship, but now it was as if the two were brothers again.

"See you later," said Martin.

"Sure."

One after another, the guests came and shook his hand. He hadn't expected the transition to be like this.

The pain was so subtle he could barely feel it. If anything of the ceremony stuck in his mind, it was Father Merser's sturdy fingers gripping the brass vessels on the altar.

Quite a few people had converted in recent years. Some with their parents' blessing, but most on their own. They were the young and not so young, and even a few old men. Five years ago a resident of the old age home had converted, a fellow of about ninety. For years he had threatened that if they didn't improve the heating, he would go to the Catholic old folks' home. People made fun of him. They didn't believe him. In the end, he carried out his threat, and Father Merser presided over the ceremony, with his customary grace.

The conversations in the reception room ebbed and flowed. People were talking about city affairs, the district, transportation, and the fate of the empire. Karl went from group to group, telling a joke or simply nodding his head.

"Permit me to congratulate you," said Hochhut the industrialist, extending the cold hand at the end of his short, stubby arm. In gymnasium Hochhut had been two classes ahead. Karl had never been fond of him. The man always made him nervous. In school Hochhut had not been much of a student, but ambition had accomplished what his brain couldn't. In fact, he had achieved the impossible, establishing a string of factories along the Danube. As if to spite everyone, he lived not in the capital, but in his native town, surrounded by friends and enemies.

The reception was supposed to last about an hour, but

it went on. In one corner people spoke energetically about the need for change in the city. Everybody knew this meant pulling down the old Jewish shops in the center of town, but no one said it in so many words. More than once in recent years the municipality had been about to condemn the district, but the merchants outsmarted the authorities, putting money in the right hands, and the plan was never carried out. Karl caught the drift of the conversation. He was familiar with the issues. His parents had owned a shop in the old market. Unprofitable, it had burdened them like a humped back. Finally, they sold it for next to nothing, to a Jewish merchant, who turned the dank cave into a thriving business.

"We're talking about the center of town."

"I understand," said Karl.

"Its former glory must be restored."

"Correct."

"The center must be elegant."

"Absolutely."

Since leaving school, Karl had worked for the municipality. His parents had wanted to send him to the university in Vienna, but in the end they simply couldn't afford to. Karl tried for a scholarship several times but failed. Without a scholarship, he had no choice but to remain in his parents' house. For a few years he worked as a trainee, and afterward he began making his way up the hierarchy. Now he had his eye on the high office of municipal secretary.

"I wish to congratulate you," said the doctor. Karl knew him well. He was a shy man, full of inhibitions, for whom school was a constant struggle. Had it not been for his parents' ambition and private tutors, he would never have graduated. So it was in medical school too. His parents worked night and day in their little shop, helping him and urging him on, but they didn't live to see him sit in his office. They had both passed away before he graduated. Karl didn't like him. For years he had avoided him. Now the doctor was standing before him, face to face. The same old Freddy, the same stooped posture, the same pallor. Neither medical school nor conversion had changed a single feature of his appearance. Karl marveled at the constancy.

"How are you, Freddy?"

"All is well. This is my wife."

Karl had never met her before. She was taller than Freddy, and thin. Traces of the peasant remained in her face, but in her expression one saw a strange blend of cunning and smugness, all because of her husband's clinic.

"You look excellent," Freddy told him.

"Same as ever," said Karl, taking a step backward.

"We would be pleased to see you in our home," said the wife.

"Delighted."

Karl knew women like this very well. While still at the gymnasium, they decided they would get a Jewish husband, no matter what. Afterward, they would mold him

9

however they wished. Now Karl noticed that something of Freddy's wife had rubbed off onto Freddy's face. To the blush of shame was added the flush of beer.

The president of the church's lay association stood against the wall, along with his assistant, glasses in hand, listening to the various conversations without mixing in. Father Merser greeted them, and they spoke about mundane affairs—lighting in the church, renovations, and the treasury, which was empty once again. Father Merser promised that in his next sermon he would not forget to remind the faithful of their duty.

Thus the reception ended. The president and his assistant left first. Then Karl's colleagues shook his hand. Freddy and his wife also approached. Martin stood to the side, waiting for the moment when he could snatch away his friend. Father Merser hugged Karl again in a fatherly way. It was clear that the tall, distinguished man was not only fond of him, but also respected him. "We shall see each other soon," Father Merser said, looking like someone who has brought a ship safely to harbor.

"Let's go," Martin called in a youthful voice, as soon as the hall was empty.

"Where to?"

"For a bite."

This could mean only one place: Big Victoria's. During their last two years of school, he and Karl went there often. At one time it had been a shabby roadside inn, where Big Victoria herself saw to everyone's needs. She was hostess, waitress, and whore combined. In their senior year she already had a helper, a girl who assisted her in all her roles. Later, Victoria fell ill and had to step aside, but she continued to keep an eye on the customers. Over the years the place had changed. Outwardly it looked respectable enough, but people knew you could find a girl in every room on the top floor.

"Just a minute," said Karl.

"What are you looking for?"

"My coat."

"It must be hanging in the coat room."

Karl opened the partition, and before his eyes the nave of the church was revealed to him in all its splendor. Candlelight and the glow of the setting sun mingled with marvelous intensity.

"Where to?" asked Karl, absentmindedly, his coat in hand.

"To restore former days," said Martin, grabbing his arm.

The two went out into the air. They were friends for any number of reasons. First of all, their parents had been friends. And then, they were in the same class and had done well in the same subjects. And they had always enjoyed each other's company. True, Martin's parents were wealthier and had sent him to study law. But Martin's position and status didn't affect their long friendship. Yet, when Martin converted, Karl felt a distance open up between them. Nevertheless, they continued to meet from time to time. Martin did well in his practice, opening up offices in nearby Celan and Schwarzhof. Meanwhile,

Karl slowly made his way through the maze of the municipal bureaucracy.

They crossed the park in the direction of the meadows and hurried along the dirt path, as they used to on their way home from school. When they reached the river, Karl spoke of his wish to sell his parents' house and buy an apartment. Martin listened intently, without interrupting.

Victoria greeted them warmly. She knew all the graduates and kept track of them. Quite a few had spent time in her broad bed. Since her illness, she no longer took them to bed, but everybody still came by for a drink now and then, or for an evening's diversion.

"It's good to see old friends together," she began.

"And how are you?" Martin allowed himself to address her familiarly.

"Out of the current, up on the bank." That was one of the sayings she had adopted in the past few years.

"And how is it up there?"

"Don't ask."

"Give us just a hint."

"Dismal, dismal. Now I'll find you a nice, quiet place, near the window. Friendship from childhood is harder than the love of women."

She knew what had happened in church that day, but she was too polite to pry. She had never been the least bit devoted to the church. Indeed, she thought the world would be better off without it. She did, however, have a certain affection for the Jews, though it was not unequivocal, and occasionally one could hear her say, "Yes, the Jews are more refined." Perhaps there was a hint of sarcasm in that compliment, but that night, in any event, her heart was not bitter. She stepped out of her booth, showed them to a quiet corner, and left them to themselves.

"I'm glad it's all over and done with," Karl said vaguely.

"Father Merser was very tactful," Martin said.

"It seemed so to me."

Karl had two glasses of cognac and immediately felt better. The sandwiches were the kind they had always served here, and he was glad to see the familiar slices of bread, as if he had returned home after a long trip.

"I love these sandwiches. They put me in a good mood," said Martin, chuckling, as he arched his back and grasped his knees.

It was after gymnasium had ended that Victoria fell ill and changed. She would send her young customers upstairs with a scowl. As if they were trying to sneak in. When she wasn't feeling well, she would grab a boy, pinch his behind, and warn him: "Don't act like a savage."

No one could forget that place. The first customers keep returning, sometimes with their wives, to remember the days when they, and the world, had been young.

"I haven't been here for a long time," said Karl.

"Neither have I."

"The elegance here is pointless. A whorehouse should look like a whorehouse, not a tea room."

"She did it to improve business." Martin tried to defend her.

They were glad to be together. The distant years returned to them with each drink. School days were not always so splendid, but it had been an intense and exhilarating time. Both boys had done excellently in mathematics and Latin. The Latin teacher, a bitter anti-Semite, would sometimes say, "Karl and Martin have brilliant minds, like all the members of their race. If only the Jews were honest, they would be a blessing to the world." The mathematics teacher, Andreas, was wittier, and it was hard to be angry at him. He would say, "Karl and Martin have Talmudic minds, though I doubt they know even a word of Hebrew."

"Yet you've been successful." The words popped out of Karl's mouth.

"Me?"

"You've succeeded in opening a couple of branch offices."

"Don't be envious of me."

Karl understood and bowed his head.

Later, Victoria approached them and said, "Will you boys be going upstairs?"

"Alas, we're no longer young," said Martin.

"I'm the one who decides that." The cognac spoke from her throat. She was so drunk that she forgot the two of them had converted and praised the Jews: "Jews," she said, "are very dear to me. First of all, they're mentschen. Lots of Jewish students have passed through here. What brilliant minds. Austria without the Jews would be an empty barrel. The Jews give Austria its balls! You can't deny it. Do you hear?"

"We hear you, loud and clear," Karl called out.

"In that case, do as Victoria says and go upstairs."

"Not today, sweetie," Martin said softly.

"As you please. I won't get in your way. You're big boys."

Later, they sat for a long while without speaking. Karl suddenly saw his mother's face. A year before her death, she had spoken often of her native village. Sometimes it seemed that she wasn't so much drawn to it but, rather, that someone from there was tugging at her. Karl's father promised that as soon as she got better, they would take their savings and go back. She had believed him at first, and even made preparations, but as her illness progressed, she realized she would never return home. Once she said to Karl, in passing, "It would be worth your while to go there, at least for the beautiful scenery." But when he asked for details, she changed her mind and said, "No, it's very old. Everything is crumbling there. You won't like it."

On their way home, Martin said, "Victoria is a very, very generous woman. I don't say that to flatter her. It's the truth."

"Yes, it's true," Karl confirmed. "Very true."

"In my youth she would sometimes take me upstairs for free."

"Me too!"

"One doesn't forget favors like that, my friend."

"You don't. That's true."

Thus they stumbled about drunk for a full hour, leaning on each other, and the friendship that had been somewhat strained in recent years was renewed. Near his front door, Karl hugged Martin and said, "It was a memorable evening. Thank you."

C H A P T E R

2

The next morning Karl woke up late and immediately got to his feet. In his sleep he had visited several forgotten regions of his past. He sat on his bed. The fine haze that had veiled his awakening gradually dispersed, but the feeling that he had been far away did not. In his sleep he was back at the gymnasium, or, to be precise, on the playing field behind the school building. In that expanse, all that had defined his youth became clear: his ability and his ambition. Unlike some, in him these qualities existed in harmony. On the playing field his body had performed wonders that could be measured with a stopwatch and a tape measure. Here he had spent many of his happiest hours. What came after was merely a tedious marching in place, and, worst of all, the feeling that life is a fierce struggle without purpose.

In the last year of her life, his mother lay in the room next to his, tormented by her illness. It was a long and cruel battle, another one of her organs destroyed every year. His father would sit by her bed, without looking at her or uttering a word. Whenever Karl sat alone with her, she would say, "If your career requires you to convert, do it. I won't be angry with you. A person has to advance. Without advancement, there is no purpose or meaning to life."

It was not her own voice speaking but clichés she had picked up in the store. All her life she had been self-reliant and hardworking, and the mistress of her own vocabulary. Now the tables seemed to have been turned: not a single word was her own. They all belonged to others. It was difficult for him to bear this change. He would work overtime, in order to avoid being at home. When he returned at night, everyone was already asleep.

Still, encounters were unavoidable. A week before her death, she had apologized in a tortured voice, "Forgive me for not sending you to Vienna. You know we didn't have the money." His mother's illness completely defeated his father. If he had ever had any will of his own, now that was gone too. Finally they had to sell the store. They sold it for nothing, to the Jewish merchant who turned the place into a flourishing business within a year.

His mother's illness had been the years of his rise in

the public administration. During those years his ties to childhood friends weakened. He became totally immersed in his work. He would return home secretively, along back alleys, and immediately plunge into sleep. His sleep had become the other face of his diligence, not sleep so much as a mere gathering of strength for the next day. Thus it went, year after year, with greater and greater momentum, like an unstoppable locomotive. His superiors appreciated his efforts and kept promoting him. Now the top was in sight.

Karl stepped over to the sink and washed his face with cold water. Contact with the water brought his mother's face to mind, when she would raise herself up in bed and say to him, "If your career requires you to convert, do it. I won't be angry with you." During her illness, lines were etched into her face indicating powerful faith. What sort of faith it was, he didn't know. He was afraid to ask. Sometimes he would encounter her open eyes, and they seemed to him like two dry streams, in whose beds unseen waters still flowed.

When he entered the silent kitchen to make a cup of coffee, he clearly remembered the evening at Victoria's, and Martin's voice saying, "Don't be envious of me." Martin's life had not gone smoothly: he had divorced twice. His first marriage had ended amicably, but the second had been difficult, even shameful. The case had gone through several appeals, and finally, to conclude the matter, he was forced to pay his ex-wife an enormous sum. Since his parents' death, his life had drifted like a ship without an anchor. In business he had done well, but his wives had gone through most of his money.

Had there been a telephone in his house, Karl would have called to say that he wasn't coming into the office. Since there wasn't, he decided to get dressed. As he did so, his room stared at him, lit as it was in every corner. From his earliest days this had been his room. From here he had left for grade school, gymnasium, and then to Vienna, where he had tried to enroll at the university. Here his hopes had blossomed, and here they had withered. Had he stayed in Vienna, surely his life would now be different, but fate had determined that he must dwell here, in this pitiful, charmless room. Every year had left a stain on the soul, and in the end all that remained was the feeling that life was gradually evaporating. After the death of his parents, that feeling had grown stronger. He would spend many long nights in the Green Eagle. Four or five glasses of cognac would dull his senses, and a kind of numbness would spread over his body. Many of his childhood friends visited the Green Eagle. Some had found success, though quite a few had not. Most had left their childhood nests and traveled off, some to the great metropolis, others to provincial cities. He alone, it seemed, remained attached to the umbilical cord, and not only to his parents' house, but to the gloomy room where he had practiced his multiplication tables.

At those chance meetings he realized that he had to move on, otherwise new horizons would never open up for him. Several times he tried to sell the house, but the sale never went through, and he was somewhat to blame. A local merchant offered him a decent sum and in cash, but Karl was repelled by the man's looks. He became stubborn and refused to go down even a penny. The merchant was astonished at his obstinacy. "This is unheard of," he said, and stalked out.

Looking back on it, Karl was glad. This was his shelter in the city, after all. Eventually, he gave up the idea of selling. The house gradually came to look shabby. This bothered him, but to paint, to renovate, was beyond his strength.

Around this time, he would occasionally run into Father Merser. Karl had known him for many years, since grade school. At the beginning of religion lessons he would announce to the class, "Will the children of the Jewish creed kindly leave the classroom now? You may play in the playground while our prayers are said." The tone of Father Merser's voice left no doubt that the world was divided into two, the higher beings who were permitted to hear the secrets of faith, and those to whom it was forbidden. At the gymnasium he occasionally substituted for the Latin teacher. Karl and Martin were both excellent students, and Father Merser would praise their knowledge. Still, it was never pleasant to meet him on the street.

Once he had come to the municipal offices to untangle his sister's affairs. For several years she had not paid her taxes. Officials had informed her that her house would be confiscated if she didn't pay them immediately. Father Merser's appearance in the municipal building embarrassed many people. Everyone went out of his way to offer assistance. The deputy mayor said sheepishly, "We apologize for the nuisance. Everything will work out for the best." Father Merser was in no hurry to leave. He greeted all the clerks and shook their hands. When Karl's turn came, he said, "It's good to see you. I sometimes think about you."

After that meeting in the municipal offices, they occasionally met in the street and spoke about city business, taxes, or culture. One night, he met Father Merser on his way home. Karl had had several drinks and was in such an expansive mood that he began reciting poems by Hölderlin. "Let's have a little walk," proposed Father Merser, taking his arm. It turned out that Father Merser was also fond of Hölderlin, and was in fact a member of the well-known society "The Eternal Hölderlin," which met once a year in Vienna. Stupidly, Karl asked him whether he might be permitted to attend the next meeting. Father Merser fell silent for a moment, then said, "Unfortunately, it is reserved for members only."

"No matter, I'll hold my own ceremony," said Karl.

The priest chuckled out loud, as if Karl had told a racy joke.

Later, they strolled along the river, and Karl told him about an unfortunate affair in which the mayor had become involved. The priest listened without comment. A distance from Karl's house, he stopped and said, "Now I'll leave you, so that people won't say that Father Merser is enticing Jews to convert."

When Karl returned home he drank some coffee and sobered up. He regretted having told the whole story about the mayor to Father Merser. He had divulged a secret, and if this were ever revealed, he would have nowhere in the city to hide. The next day Karl saw the priest again. Father Merser was preoccupied with his sick cousin, who was in terrible pain and wanted to die. He spoke freely, like a man opening his heart to a friend.

The next time they ran into each other, Karl said, "Father Merser, I would like to speak with you about something."

"Gladly. Let's meet at my house on Tuesday. Tuesdays are my music days. We'll listen and talk."

Karl didn't know why he had made the appointment. Then he remembered that the mayor seemed to be avoiding him lately.

On Tuesday, Father Merser and his sister Clara greeted Karl. The sister, who was wearing a tight black dress, resembled a certain well-known actress who had recently been found in bed with an under-age boy.

They sat in the salon as the maid served tea and cheese cakes. Then a young girl entered, introducing herself as Elsa Blauber, and asked permission to play Mozart. While she played, Father Merser reminisced about his childhood. It turned out that not only had he and his father studied in the gymnasium but also his grandfather and great-grandfather. The Mersers leaned toward science, and only a few of them had entered the priesthood. At home, sitting beside the blue stove, some of his splendor was gone, and he seemed like an ordinary person. At that meeting he told a few jokes, some of them rather risqué. His sister laughed and wildly threw her head about. "I can't take it," she cried out.

They parted pleasantly, like old friends, without the priest ever asking what Karl had wanted to discuss. From then on when they met they would exchange just a few words, but sometimes they stood and spoke for quite a while.

Martin he saw frequently. Martin let him know that he thought that the position of municipal secretary would be offered to him only if a certain obstacle were removed. Karl knew what he meant, but sometimes it's difficult to discuss private matters even with childhood friends. They drank and drank some more, yet avoided that sensitive subject.

Nonetheless, it had begun. Sometimes Karl would find himself immersed in conversation with the priest, mainly about poetry, but sometimes also about matters of faith. The priest did not conceal his opinion that only the church was capable of binding together faith and art. That was its power and its uniqueness.

In fairness to Father Merser it must be said: he never pressured or coaxed, and once he even said to Karl, "You must consider this very carefully. One doesn't convert frivolously."

Karl went to the priest's house on several Tuesdays. The ceremony always followed the same pattern: the sister, afternoon tea and cakes, and finally, the same girl, always introducing herself as Elsa Blauber, and requesting permission to play Mozart sonatas.

Eventually, Karl took the initiative and read the New Testament. At first it seemed that the gates of light had opened before him. But the more he read, the more repelled he was by all the miracles repeated over and over. He made no attempt to conceal this from Father Merser. "This is the task of faith," the priest said.

The struggle was decided elsewhere. Night after night his mother would appear in his dreams and tell him, as she had in her lifetime, "If your career requires you to convert, do it." Now it was clear to him that her words had not been spontaneous but rather well considered. "I won't be angry with you." That sentence was especially important to him now, for it meant: there are unpleasant things that we must do, and the sooner we do them, the better it is for all of us.

His father made no pronouncements, neither in life nor after his death. As in life, now, too, his father sat squinting ironically. When all was said and done, he had hated both practicality, and religion. On the holidays he used to go to synagogue, but not with joy. The church revolted him. He sometimes said as much with a word or two. Those isolated words had stuck in Karl's mind like stakes.

The nights were dark and teeming with years and places. In gymnasium, principle had been more important to him than practice. Principle above all. Life without principles was degenerate, he and Martin would tell themselves again and again.

I will resign and travel to a small town and live there as a free man, Karl whispered to himself. But another voice, stronger, or perhaps coarser, said to him: A man doesn't abandon a secure position that he's worked at for twenty years. In his dreams, school friends appeared, Jews who used to visit his house, relatives who came from far off, his Aunt Franzi and her friends. Like him, they too had been forced to make difficult decisions. Finally, a voice shouting from within him decided, shouting like the master sergeant who used to drill his soldiers not far from the gymnasium: "Don't think—*march!*"

One evening he saw Father Merser walking down Lilac Lane. For a moment he wanted to ignore him, but he couldn't. He ran to catch up with the priest.

"I've decided," he said, panting from his run.

"I'm pleased," said the priest, in his fatherly voice. For some reason that night he didn't look like a clergyman, but a surgeon whose patient had finally decided to undergo a risky operation.

"I was in doubt," said Karl.

"Naturally."

"And now I'm relieved."

"I'm pleased."

Father Merser grasped him with both hands and said, "We'll see each other on Tuesday. Music is a good foundation for new thought."

That same night he informed Martin of his decision. Martin didn't appear to be especially pleased. He was immersed in his work and the news didn't seem to penetrate. "That's good," he told Karl distractedly.

"It wasn't easy for me," Karl confessed.

"I did it with a stroke of my hand."

Later, they drank. The cognac raised Karl's spirits, and he spoke at length about the vivid dreams that had tormented him in recent nights. Martin was lost within himself and made only a few inconsequential comments.

Martin continued to drink, and the back of his neck turned red. That night, for the first time, Karl noticed a tic in Martin's face. He was about to speak to him, to implore him to stop drinking, when Martin, apparently sensing this, spoke first. "Why don't you convert to Christianity?" he asked.

"I've decided to. I *told* you that I decided to," Karl answered impatiently.

"I don't believe you."

"Why not?"

"You always change your mind."

"You're mistaken."

"I'm not mistaken. I know you very well."

"Why argue about this? I tell you, I've made up my mind."

"I don't believe you."

Karl knew that Martin was drunk and that his insults were just symptoms of his own troubles. Still, it was hard for him to bear.

"I'm going home." Karl rose to his feet.

"I won't conceal the truth from you," Martin shouted.

"What truth is that?" Karl said without moving.

"You know very well."

"I've had enough," said Karl, fleeing.

Karl never discussed that evening with Martin again, but his friend's drunken face would not fade from his mind. That dear, generous Martin, who had been bound to him for years, and whom he would always love, had appeared that evening as a frightening incarnation of himself.

A full month passed between the decision and the conversion. It was a long month. In the office, people knew of his decision, but no one spoke openly of it. Still, his ear caught a whisper: "Jews are willing to do anything, even to convert." That was one of the typists, a bitter, unfortunate woman for whom the Jews were thorns in her flesh. But this time she was merely parroting the words of her boss, an official at Karl's level who was also vying for the secretaryship.

For years, Karl had had his eye on that post. But now that he was close to achieving it, he felt anxious. Perhaps because his parents were dead. Who was there to be proud of him? Only parents felt such pride. Others felt only envy or resentment.

Once again he thought of Martin. After Martin's first divorce, it had seemed to Karl that he was recovering, looking younger, even. But that was an illusion. When he met him for a drink in the Green Eagle, he was curled up like a sick animal. After his second marriage, a change was apparent in his face. His ironic expression had disappeared. His features thickened. Nothing of the youthful, athletic Martin remained. Even his vigorous step was gone. His gait had become clumsy, like that of a bull in a field. Karl used to avoid him, but he didn't always succeed. Sometimes he would run into him at night, in the company of a disgusting whore. He looked like a janitor in a general store, rather than a respected lawyer.

C H A P T E R

3

The next day, upon awakening, he sensed that he had just heard a few clear sentences spoken, but he could not register what they were. The morning light crossed the dining room lengthwise. Since his parents' death, the house had changed beyond recognition. Not in obvious ways. All the objects still stood in their regular places. But the silence showed that their souls were no more.

While he was staring at the dish cupboard, Gloria rose up before his eyes, as if borne upon the waves of the Danube. "Gloria!" he called out. After his father's death she had fled the house and had not returned. For more than thirty years she had worked in the house, a devoted and loyal servant in days of joy and of grief. And when that accursed illness had invaded his mother, Gloria never left her bedside. Later, she had cared for his father the same way until his last day. During the seven days of mourning, she had served black coffee to those offering condolences. Immediately afterward, without saying a word, she vanished. For Karl, her disappearance was bound up with his parents' death. As if she had gone after them to that unknown land. He had considered looking for her in her native village, but he kept putting the trip off, immersing himself ever deeper in his work, and then in his frequent meetings with Father Merser and the conversion. His thoughts of Gloria slowly sank into oblivion. True, it was not a total disappearance. Her image would occasionally float up before him in the street, or sometimes even in the house. He became used to these apparitions, and they no longer disturbed him.

He had not spoken with Gloria since his mother's illness. Even before then, in his gymnasium days, he had not spoken with her much. Both Martin and Freddy knew her well, but whenever he thought to ask about her, his tongue would cleave to the roof of his mouth.

There was another hidden pain: during her illness, his mother had expressed several wishes that echoed in his heart like the clauses of a will. Among other things she had said, "Watch over our Gloria." Every word that left her mouth at that time seared him now. The clauses of her will seemed like accusations to him. In just one area Karl emerged unblemished: financial support. After his parents had used up their savings on doctors and medicines, Karl transferred his assets to them—everything he had. His mother had been moved by his generosity, and every time he entered the house or stood by her bed, she would say, "God will reward you for this mercy." In that turmoil, Gloria was lost. She had vanished.

On his way to the office, Karl was stopped by a tall man. It was as if the man was trying to prevent Karl from leaping over a fence. At first Karl was taken aback, but then he recognized the broad, bony hand that used to handle old maps and globes with such authority. This elegant man from the north had been Karl's geography teacher.

"How are you, Karl?" he said in his familiar, warm voice.

"Excellent. How good it is to see you."

"I've heard you're doing well."

"From whom, Herr Professor?"

He had been one of the decent teachers, broadminded and humble. He would breathe life into every lesson, and everything he brought into the classroom, even trivial objects, would gain a kind of spiritual essence. His ancestors had come from Sweden, and the blue in his eyes glistened as if taken from the North Sea. He was especially fond of Jews, wasn't sure why. He had once spent an entire year in the Carpathians seeking out rural synagogues. With great precision he had documented and photographed each one he found. He had shown Karl and Martin the photograph album. He spoke passionately about those miniature temples that looked like rickety shacks from the outside. "If you're going to pray, that's how you should do it, not in the grandiose kitsch that stares out at you from every city church." His words had astounded them. They had never heard a gentile praise the Jews, and especially not their religion. They were fourteen then, a time when the wonders of geometry interested them more than the mysteries of faith. Judaism appeared to them in their parents' image: merchants standing beside the cash box, anxious about the daily receipts.

Now Karl stood before him like a negligent student—who instead of doing his homework properly had copied whole pages out of the encyclopedia. He was embarrassed before this elegant old gentleman who had harbored such love for the Jewish faith and had even learned Hebrew, to read the Bible and Hasidic books in their original language.

"I'm going back to the Carpathians soon. There are still more synagogues to survey. A man of my age must hurry. Time doesn't stand still, my dear fellow."

"You're still possessed, I see."

"Have you ever heard of the Baal-Shem-Tov?"

"No, sir."

"You must read Buber's writing about him. Magnificent things."

Karl was embarrassed, as if exposed in broad daylight. The thought that his old teacher, Mr. Zauber, was now traveling to the place where his own ancestors had lived, because he found that the Jewish faith was superior to that of the high and splendid churches—this thought scorched him, and he said, "I must read it, for these were my forefathers."

"Hasidism is a great religious phenomenon that the world has not properly recognized."

"Are the Jews themselves aware of this treasure?" Karl asked with amusement.

"Sometimes you don't know what's in your own house. Have you ever been in the Carpathians?"

"No."

"One must go there to see the true servants of God."

"What distinguishes them?"

"Their gestures."

"Strange," said Karl. "It's hard for me to imagine Jews devoted to faith."

"Really?" Zauber was astonished.

"Jews are so skeptical by nature."

"Then you must travel to the Carpathians and change your views."

"When are you leaving?" asked Karl.

"Soon, very soon."

"Can we see each other again?" Karl asked.

"I suppose so," Zauber answered vaguely, as if he had been asked an intimate question.

In the office everything was in its place. The clerks greeted him and said good morning, and in his out box was a stack of letters awaiting his signature. On the desk lay a few messages and also the day's schedule, prepared by his secretary. Within a few moments he was totally absorbed in his work. He had known this place since his youth. He was at home in every file, in every labyrinth. No one dared to challenge the power of his memory.

While the day flowed at its usual pace, one of the clerks, a woman, approached and congratulated him on his conversion. She was middle-aged and of middle rank and did her job with a kind of obsessive pedantry. Still, she always managed to make mistakes and botch things, and this time too she made Karl furious. It's a private matter, he was about to reprimand her, but of course he didn't. He politely thanked her.

"What a happy occasion!" she erupted, annoying him further.

"What?" He couldn't ignore her comment.

"You see, my parents were devout Christians."

"So what?" he said, unable to restrain himself.

"Excuse me, I suppose I got carried away," she said and returned to her desk.

It was clear that not only she but the entire office— the apprentices and the archivists, the cleaners and the porters—had all heard the ringing of the church bells on Wednesday. One woman said, "Soon there won't be any Jews left. Father Merser is baptizing them one after the other. But I don't trust them. A Jew, even after he's been baptized, is still a Jew. He'll always cheat you or betray you."

The thought that such a woman would mock him made his blood boil. Since he was only used to expressing his thoughts in memoranda, he reached out, took pen and paper, and wrote: From now on, no one will interfere in anyone else's personal business. Privacy must be respected. But his well-trained hand immediately knew that one doesn't draft memoranda on subjects like this, and he stopped.

Aside from this small unpleasantness, the day went smoothly. His meetings were all on time, and he saw everyone he needed to. All that remained was an appointment with an unfortunate woman clerk whose work was not up to snuff. Her fate was in his hands.

The woman arrived on time and started out by saying, "I know that I have been seriously negligent on two occasions. But I promise that this will be the last time. If anything else happens, I won't ask for mercy again."

Karl bowed his head, and she continued. "I'm a single woman. I have no one in the city, and my salary isn't just for me but for my sick father and mother. Forgive me for allowing myself to speak openly. Whatever you decide, I must at least speak the truth."

"Yes, of course." Karl tried to be brief.

"Forgive me, sir. There's more. I have a daughter from my wretched marriage. She's sick and hospitalized in a sanatorium. I don't pay for this. Merciful people do. But every month I buy her a little present and put it in the mail. Nothing expensive, just a trinket. But I know how she looks forward to these treats. That's all, sir. No more, but also no less."

"I see," said Karl, rising to his feet. "I'm writing the

following: Mrs. Hoffmayer admits her errors and promises not to be negligent again. I have accepted her word. She will not be discharged at this time."

"Thank you, sir, with all my heart."

"From now on you must be careful," he warned her.

"May God watch over you like the apple of his eye," she said, bowing her head the way she might before a statue in church.

Suddenly, Karl remembered his family's housemaid from the days of his childhood, the year or two before Gloria's arrival, a sturdy, ugly woman named Brunhilde. She stole shamelessly. But when she was caught, she would weep and beg forgiveness, swearing on her parents' lives that she would never steal again. She was caught several times, and in the end she was fired. The next day she packed her belongings and cursed the world and everything in it. Nor did she hold her tongue as she was leaving. "You can't trust the Jews," she said. "They'll always betray you."

C H A P T E R

4

Then summer came and the sky was bright and cloud-less. After work he would stroll on Salzburg Boulevard, a long street that he loved. He always hoped he would find Gloria there. In his childhood they used to set out from here for the open fields beside the river. Gloria loved the place because of the tall trees and all the birds. Here she showed him her magic: squirrels and birds would nibble seeds from her hands.

Though he longed to see her, he had postponed the trip to her native village. For some reason he wanted to consult Martin first, even though he knew that Martin always drank cognac in the afternoon and his mind wouldn't be clear. Still, it was important for him to hear his advice. Karl had once asked his secretary to find out the distance from Neufeld to Schenetz. The secretary brought an atlas, studied the map and the index, but found no mention of the village. Strangely, Karl was relieved. It was as if he had been granted a postponement.

Images of the past overwhelmed him. Silent and bright, they filled his sleep: his father and mother in the kitchen, the eternal kitchen, conjuring memories. After an hour of this, the Carpathian Mountains, where they had been born, invaded the narrow kitchen, filling it till there was no room to breathe. Then their faces took on a different character. A glimmer of their fathers' faith illuminated their brows. Not only did their faces change, but also their language, as if German were excised from their mouths, and another language, somehow related to it, rose up and made their lips speak. It was clear to Karl that this was their true language, and only in its words could they express the fullness of their hearts.

"I don't understand a word," laughed the little boy Karl, spreading out his tiny palms.

"It's Yiddish," said the mother, picking him up.

"Whose language is that?"

"The Jews'."

His parents had stopped speaking their language, and only at night, when Karl was sound asleep, did they return to it. Since childhood he had harbored fondness for its sounds. Often he would ask, "Mother, why don't you talk the secret language?"

"What do you mean?"

"Why don't you talk the Jews' language?"

"We must speak German. In Austria everyone speaks German."

He loved his parents' secret language, as he did the pretty girls who entered the store. The Czech girls were the prettiest of all. They were buxom, and the braids on their backs were thick and black. And their happiness contrasted with his parents' misery. Earning a living had darkened their faces. Karl's mother would torment his father with many stabbing words. His father would bow his head and silently accept his shame. But sometimes he couldn't contain himself. His expression would suddenly change, his voice would thunder, and his face would take on an evil cast. In time, that expression too changed. Instead of burning anger an ironic smile grew up, reflecting a strange mixture of contempt and resignation. It was difficult to be in his parents' company.

Occasionally, as if from oblivion, an uncle of his would emerge from the Carpathians. A tall man, thin, with a bent back. In a moment the house would change. The man would sit and, in a hushed and monotonous voice, tell stories about life's shame and struggles. Then the secret language would become the language of pain.

And Gloria again. After years of submissive housework, her face had lost its ruddiness, and a kind of tormented tenderness settled over it. She worked from morning until late at night, but on sabbaths and holidays, when she sat at the table or by the window, they clearly saw that the gloom of the house had seeped into her. Her rustic dialect was not lost, though here and there new words infiltrated the speech she had brought with her. The house belonged to her more than to his parents. She shaped its center and its corners. Everything was kneaded by her hands. Karl too belonged to her. She washed him and fed him. When his parents came home from the store at night, he was already fast asleep.

He met Martin once a week, on Mondays. At first their renewed friendship had a fresh taste, but soon it lost its power. The closeness had been exhausted years ago, and only embers that refused to burst into flame were left.

They sat in silence, and only after a few drinks would Martin's heart open. He talked about his marriages and divorces and about how much money he had wasted on nothing. The subject came up every Monday. Karl was so familiar with the monologue, all the intimate details, that it disgusted him. He regretted that Martin was revealing things that should have been passed over in silence. Martin blamed his parents. If he had studied what he wanted to, his fate would have been different. But his parents had insisted—law and only law. They did not speak about their conversions, as if they had agreed not to.

Martin was the only person with whom he met outside the office. Everyone was polite to him, but no one except Freddy invited him home. And even Freddy stopped inviting him. Karl had put him off too many times with weak excuses. Freddy's submissive face depressed him, and he couldn't stand his wife. He had hoped that after his conversion people's hearts would open, and that he would be invited to many homes, to parties and banquets. This hope was not fulfilled. People were cordial to him in the office, but he remained at a social distance. Once he mentioned this to Martin, whose reply was short: "So it seems to you." Since then he hadn't mentioned it again. After two or three drinks, Martin was no longer able to listen, only to talk about the same old pain.

Without realizing it they returned to Victoria's tavern. Every time Karl tried to discuss Gloria's disappearance, his voice choked. To mention her name in this dissolute place would be an act of desecration. Finally, he overcame his inhibition and asked, "Do you remember Gloria?"

"Who?"

"Gloria."

"That name means nothing to me."

That was the end of that matter.

But Victoria was pleased with them. Every time they appeared, she would come out to them, her face aglow. She would sit with them and tell them about her childhood. Her father and mother had been rough people, but her eldest sister had been even worse. She had forced Victoria to work like a slave, and on Sundays, she dragged her to church.

One evening, in her drunkenness, she turned to Karl and said, "Karl, why did you convert?"

"Because I wanted to be a Christian. Didn't I do the right thing?"

"Jews should stay Jewish. That's the right thing for them."

"Why?"

"Because a Jew is a Jew. He mustn't change. He becomes ugly if he changes."

"And if he wants to change?"

"He mustn't."

"Will it harm him?"

"It will harm us all."

"Should I take back the conversion?"

"In my opinion, yes."

"And what would be the good of that?"

"You'll be Karl again," she said, sticking her tongue out at him.

Martin responded strangely to Victoria's words. First he burst out laughing. Then he said, "I don't understand you, Victoria. You're a smart woman. Why are you making him brood? Karl did the right thing, and he should be congratulated." Victoria stuck her tongue out at him too.

Martin was as drunk as usual, and on the way home he cursed the evening and Victoria, and every whore in whose bed he had ever wasted a night. Then he began speaking of "inspiration" for a reason that Karl could not fathom. Karl wanted to ask what he meant but realized that one doesn't ask a drunk about his drunkenness.

They passed through the dark streets, past city hall, past the gymnasium, and past the shuttered stores. Karl held Martin's arm, which was limp. His whole body was unsteady.

"Gravity doesn't seem to be working on you, Martin. What's the matter?"

"What do you want?" asked Martin.

"I said the force of gravity doesn't seem to be working on you. You're floating all over the place."

"I abolished the force of gravity, didn't you know?"

"How did you do that?"

"It's very simple. You just raise your arms and soar. Let go of me, I'll show you."

Karl obliged and Martin fell on his face. Karl tried to pick him up but he couldn't. Martin rose to his knees and groaned, "I'm soaring, I'm soaring."

"We're not far from home. Come on, we can make it," Karl tried to encourage him.

"I don't have to go home."

"You have to sleep," Karl said to him the way one talks to a drunk.

He held Martin's arm firmly and brought him to his doorstep. At first Martin refused to go in, but finally he agreed. The living room was spacious, with clothing and papers scattered everywhere. He had moved into the house after his last divorce.

C  H  A  P  T  E  R

5

On Tuesday the bells rang. Karl heard them and knew that someone else had converted. At first they sounded like Sunday bells, but then he realized his mistake. These bells rang with holiday spirit. He remembered that he had heard in the corridor that Elsa Ring was about to be baptized. One of the secretaries, a trim woman with a hollow voice, had whispered the news about Elsa to her friend. They laughed tartly, as if they were gossiping about an adulterous affair. He started to reproach them but was in a hurry to get to the conference room for a meeting. Later the incident faded from his memory.

The meeting was long and tedious, strewn with many

documents. In the beginning he concentrated, listening and intervening, but as time passed he lost interest. Then the resentment that had been hidden within him for a long time flared up. He was angry at Father Merser for baptizing people wholesale. Father Merser lost his judgment when conversion was at issue. Everyone was fair game for him, from minors to old people. Besides, he made his actions public, so that everyone rejoiced at the expense of those left behind. Suddenly, he felt the flaw in his own conversion. Before the ceremony, he had asked Father Merser to keep it private. The priest nodded, and Karl thought he would respect his wishes. But when the time came, the whole city turned out to celebrate, and the bells sounded as if for a feast day.

Elsa Ring was a woman of no simple beauty. Her nose, thin and sharp, grew sharper still when she was angry, and with the lightning of her eyes, it became an absolute blade on her face, giving it a noble wildness. Once people had predicted great things for her in the theater. They said that Stefan Zweig had seen her on the stage and was enchanted. For a few years she had studied in Vienna. Then she performed all over the world. From time to time echoes of her successes were heard. She was the secret pride of the Jewish merchants of Neufeld. Then nothing was heard of her for years. Still, the magic spirit named Elsa Ring continued to haunt Karl's house.

Elsa was Aunt Franzi's good friend, and both of them had taken off from this stuffy nest for the great wide world. More had been expected of Elsa Ring. Perhaps because she was taller and sturdier. Perhaps because people remembered that she had once slapped the assistant principal of the gymnasium in the face for calling one of her friends a Jew. There was no shortage of scandals. The two girls smoked in public, declaring that life was not a prison, but a breath of fresh air. People in the city despised them, called them bad names, but the Jewish merchants were secretly proud and expected great things of them.

Elsa had married a well-known actor, but the marriage was not happy. After the divorce she left the theater and wandered from city to city. Then, without warning, she returned to Neufeld. She was about forty then, and still very pretty. The town held its breath. Her mother, who lived in an old-age home, got out of bed and said, "There are miracles in the world." That very week Elsa bought a house outside of town, near the flour mill, and shut herself up in it.

During their gymnasium years, Karl and Martin used to walk as far as that abandoned, marvelous corner and sit on a hill in the hopes of catching a glimpse of her beside a window. Once they found her sitting in the garden. But when she noticed them, she folded her chair and fled inside. Still, they would return to that spot to commune with her, if only from a distance.

One evening she astonished the town by appearing in Friedrich Square. She was rushing to the post office when a thug, a waiter in a tavern, called her names. For a moment it appeared that she would ignore him, but when he called her a dirty Jew, she raised her head defiantly and proclaimed, "Indeed I am a Jew, and I am proud of it. And if yours is the face of Austria, I hereby declare myself a Jew for all eternity." Alone she faced a crowd, standing tall and speaking with fervor, but without fear. Karl saw her then from up close. A strangeness suffused her face. After that she was not seen again, and people stopped talking about her, even the merchants in the center. Once he heard one of the merchants say, "Elsa Ring never existed. She was only a legend." This remark made Karl angry. Elsa Ring was, after all, bound up with the memory of his Aunt Franzi.

Once he happened to hear about the Ring family's wanderings from a merchant. Like most of the town's merchants, they too had come from Galicia and tried their luck here. But fortune had not favored them. Had it not been for Elsa, who began to make her way on the stage at an early age, they would have starved. Her father lay in bed most of the day and accused himself: because of me our good Elsa is keeping bad company. In his grief, he lost his sanity. The merchant told the story, unfurling the details like a coarse piece of cloth. Karl loathed his tone. Unable to restrain himself, he shouted, "That's no way to speak!"

Later, her housekeeper made it known that she had changed greatly. No one came to visit her, and letters had also stopped arriving. Several merchants collected money and sent it to her. Elsa returned the envelope unopened. But her name still refused to be erased. They said she was about to come back to life and reconquer the stage. They said she had always been reclusive, that she needed time to herself to prepare for great roles.

During the past year, Father Merser's visits to her house had become more frequent. Everyone saw him walking toward her home, but no one believed he could persuade her to convert. "Elsa Ring is a proud Jew and a woman of principle. She can't be bought with fancy words," they said.

Finally, reality slapped them in the face. On September 8 they saw Father Merser cross the avenue, pushing a wheelchair before him. At first they thought he was bringing his cousin Regina to the clinic. Then the truth struck like lightning: it was Elsa Ring, or rather what was left of her, sitting in the narrow wheelchair, wrapped in a brown blanket. She was being pushed by Father Merser along the street that led directly to the great Church of St. George.

Karl was in his office. It was a day crammed with meetings that left him exhausted. He was overcome with fatigue when he heard the bells sound.

"What's happened?" he asked himself.

"Elsa Ring is converting today," the secretary answered without raising her head.

"What?"

"She has been very ill in the past year. Now the Church will take care of her."

"Hard to believe."

It pained him to think that Elsa Ring's life had come to this. For a moment he thought of sending his secretary

49

off on an errand so he could write a long letter to Elsa. Karl did not express emotions easily. But suddenly words he hadn't used for years shone in his mind. We have sinned against you, Elsa, he wanted to write, and we deserve no forgiveness. We didn't know how to love you, and we didn't come to your aid in a difficult time. We are all petty criminals, hiding by night in the dens of the Green Eagle. But not for long, if I may make a promise. Yes, we have converted, but we are still mentschen.

He thought of going to the church and asking Father Merser to let him take Elsa home. He thought if he went to her house, it would change his life, that it would truly be reformed. This thought pulled him out of the office and propelled him into the street. Unfortunately, several converts, crude careerists, were also heading toward the church. On the spot he decided: better the tavern.

He crossed the path of pines, circled the main street, and abruptly entered the back door of the Green Eagle. After two drinks a kind of oblivion cushioned his brain. The third drink deepened that oblivion, and he remembered nothing of the day's turmoil.

While he was sitting alone in the corner, a man approached him, a leather merchant, to complain about the sewers on his street. Karl wanted to say this wasn't his responsibility, that there was a municipal department that took care of such things. Besides, these weren't his working hours. He had the right to an hour for himself. Nevertheless, he spoke politely to the man and promised that the next day he would look into the matter. But the man, who was drunk and belligerent, demanded an explicit promise, a demand which Karl did not reject out of hand. Before Karl knew it, the rude merchant was joined by his cousin, who was also drunk. Immediately, the cousin declared that the Jews only take care of themselves.

"Really. That's news to me," said Karl, without raising his voice.

"Let the Jews mind their own business and stay out of public affairs."

"Don't speak that way," said Karl, no longer able to restrain himself.

"I'll say whatever I want," boasted the cousin.

Karl felt strength flowing into his arms, the kind he felt as a student, before swimming or running. No one in school had dared to raise a hand against him or Martin. They were tall and strong and weren't afraid to fight when they had to.

"I suggest you speak politely," Karl said softly, driving the man over the edge. He mocked, insulted, and finally, for some reason, called Karl a provocateur. Wanting to see how far he would go, or if anyone would take his side, Karl kept his composure. No one intervened. The customers stayed put, watching the dispute with vulgar curiosity.

After a number of futile explanations, attempts at courtesy and patience, Karl stood up and punched the man in his drunken face. When he attempted to hit Karl back, he collapsed. From the floor, he threatened that someday justice would be done, but Karl couldn't listen to his ranting anymore. He paid and left.

On the way home he met no one. The tranquility of night was spread over the houses and gardens. Only very late, in bed, he saw Elsa Ring again, as he had in his youth. Her face was pure and unblemished. He felt sadness for that purity, which now had been sullied.

C H A P T E R

6

In early October, Karl's promotion was brought before the senior appointments committee. On that committee sat two former municipal secretaries, the deputy mayor, and, representing the local manufacturers' association, Hochhut the industrialist. The matter had been languishing in file baskets for months, and now it was finally being brought to light.

He had been with the municipality for seventeen years, since finishing his gymnasium studies, and he had worked in every department, from finance to culture. There was no part of the administration with which he was not familiar. He knew the things that were visible and those that were concealed, the staff, the donors, and of course the elected officials. It was clear to everyone that he was the front-runner for the job. Of course, there were a few other senior officials who submitted their candidacy, but everyone knew that no one had experience like Karl's.

Still, ever since submitting his name, he had been uneasy. He kept examining himself in the context of the others. For instance, he discovered that the senior official Brautreben had managed a factory before joining the finance department. Everyone agreed that the finance department was the most complicated one, and for two years he had succeeded in running it well. He was married, had children, and was a member of the parents' committee. Not only was he a good official but a concerned citizen. Karl saw virtue in every one of the other candidates, and he began to wonder if the conversion would really be viewed as a point in his favor.

Without realizing it, he became suspicious of Hochhut the industrialist. Karl had known him for years. They had sat together on committees more than once. But Karl had always felt a certain discomfort in his company. Hochhut had converted many years before. Over the years he had acquired all the mannerisms of wood manufacturers. These were men shaped by their work with log rafts and sawmills. There had never been any friction between him and Hochhut. In fact, just two months earlier Karl had authorized two building permits submitted by a contracting company in which Hochhut was a partner. Still, the feeling that Hochhut was going to block his appointment grew stronger and took root in him.

The next morning he rose, determined to dispel the suspicion. The office was incredibly busy. The files came one after the other. He ate lunch with a childhood friend who was visiting the town. The hours passed slowly but not without pleasure. Only toward evening, on his way home, did he imagine Hochhut's face again. It was a strong face, resolved against the appointment. Karl felt that if the appointment didn't go through, he would have to resign, leave town, and start another life elsewhere. He regretted his youth, years wasted in this out-of-the-way place, friends he had abandoned, and his parents, from whom he had been estranged.

Again, dreams overwhelmed him. For some reason he thought that if he could find Gloria, everything would be put right and the appointment would come through. His sleep became the realm of extended searches, in which his mother, Martin, and senior officials of the municipality took part. These dreams had a clarity that invaded his day. After work he would wander for hours along the Salzburg Boulevard, mulling them over.

Not far from the boulevard were several seedy bars where Gloria occasionally went. "The peasant in me still needs it," she would joke. His mother knew of this weakness and forgave her. In fact, if she saw her in a dark mood, she would say, "Gloria, why don't you go have a drink?"

One evening he entered one of the bars and asked about Gloria.

"We haven't seen her in a long time."

"Where is she?"

"Probably with the Jews. She's always with them."

There was a meanness in the bartender's voice, and Karl wanted to punch him in the face, but he was too gripped by revulsion at the whole scene. The place seemed like a stinking swamp, and he feared that if he took one more step, he would sink.

This wasn't the city he had once loved. From every corner a drunken or wicked face popped up. He lost faith in the possibility of doing good and being rewarded for it. He saw the other officials as a buzzing swarm of bees that stood in the way of the public good. He knew them individually, by name, and he knew what went on in each of their heads. He felt they would never appoint him to the secretaryship. He knew too much, or so they thought. Nor was conversion a panacea. In fact, it had come to seem harmful to him. As if the cover had been removed from some forgotten hiding place. Now anyone could peek in.

Finally, he entered the White Horse and downed three cognacs. His heart opened as he sat with the woman who owned the place. Kirzl had gone to grade school with him. At the gymnasium they were together for just two years. Her father hadn't allowed her to finish. A daughter has to help at home. She was short, pretty, and attractive. When she was seventeen an estate owner fell in love with her and they married. But it didn't last long, so she returned to her father's house and the bar. Sometimes she would come to see Karl at the municipal building, and he would help her.

"Have you seen Gloria?" he asked.

"She hasn't been here for a year."

"I'm planning to go to her village to see what happened to her."

"You're doing the right thing. She's a precious woman."

Kirzl was a good soul who was surrounded by suffering. If she could help, she did. Old men, paupers, and sick people came to her bar. More than a few of them ate there for free. Over the years her face had lost its healthy glow, her body had become gaunt and her fingers swollen. But the innocence of her childhood still sparkled in her eyes.

During gymnasium she had hardly uttered a word. Studying was as hard for her as splitting the Red Sea. Doing homework, she would bang her head against the wall. Over the years the voice within her taught her to listen to people. Now she focused on Karl. But he wasn't talking. The few words in his mouth had dried up. So she told him about the place and the people. Once she had spoken only of herself. Now the bar was her life. "I never ask people for what they can't give," she said. "A person who expects love ends up lonely. Even parents don't know how to love their children . . ." The peasant girl, who had failed mathematics and Latin, now had an advantage over him.

Kirzl sensed his sadness, poured him a drink and said, "Let's have another. This cognac is cheap, but good." Karl sat and looked at her. The blows her father and husband had given her were stamped on her face, but they hadn't injured her soul.

"Are you angry with your father?" he finally asked.

"Not anymore. He suffered in his own way."

"It's hard for us to reconcile with our parents, isn't it?" Karl asked.

"It's true. For many years I hated my father bitterly, and didn't like my mother either."

"My mother died a very difficult death," the words left Karl's mouth.

"I forgave them," Kirzl said.

"How?"

"Faith commands us to forgive, does it not?"

"My parents lived all those years with a feeling of guilt for not doing enough for me."

"That happens only among Jews. With us, parents accuse the children."

"Interesting."

"Now that they're no longer here, why bother them?"

"You're right."

Later, he wandered along Salzburg Boulevard and followed the river until midnight. Sitting with Kirzl had drawn him out of the swamp, but his feeling that that simple woman had some kind of advantage over him did not fade. Neither his studies nor life had taught him to live properly. His life was passing in a haze of hopeless anxiety.

# CHAPTER

# 7

In October he saw neither Martin nor Freddy. Once he glimpsed Martin from a distance, staggering and barely staying on his feet. He wanted to approach him but couldn't bring himself to. Their last meetings had been awkward and unpleasant. Martin had made remarks that had hurt him. He avoided Freddy altogether. He would run into friends from childhood in the halls of the municipal building, but he didn't talk to them long. One thing occupied his mind without letup: the appointment. As if to drive himself even more crazy, he occasionally saw Hochhut, who did not seem the least bit ill at ease. He stood at the entrance or in the hallway, chatting with contractors and senior officials. If a woman happened across his path, he didn't begrudge her a compliment. But those casual ways seemed like a ruse to Karl. He kept his distance from Hochhut.

For some reason he thought the appointment would surely slip through his fingers unless he fetched Gloria from her native village. Yet he put off the trip from week to week.

One night he realized that he had to break through the barrier and address Hochhut directly. But when he awoke the next morning, the idea seemed more senseless to him than the trip to distant Schenetz.

"You mustn't worry," said Kirzl. "Worry shortens your life. If the appointment goes through—fine. If not, maybe it's for the best."

"The whole thing angers me," said Karl, unable to contain himself.

"We're commanded to love without anger."

"To love whom?"

"Those close to us, at least."

"No one wants me."

"God loves you, Karl, as if you were His only child," said Kirzl, her eyes shining.

Her faith shook him. Karl felt an emptiness in his body, as if his will had been drained.

When he left the White Horse, he forced himself to walk for a long while along Salzburg Boulevard to the river. The river was serene, its water still. At first Kirzl's words seemed simple and straightforward. But the more he walked, the more he felt that there was a trace of self-righteousness in what she said. Years ago, someone had said to him, "Life is a stream of confusions and torments, and it's best to say so forthrightly." Now he couldn't remember the circumstances.

When he returned home after midnight he found a telegram saying, "Franzi Hübner has passed away. The funeral will leave from her home at twelve o'clock." He put the paper down on the table and lit the kitchen light. When he looked at it again, he had no doubt; the old ghosts had returned to life.

Aunt Franzi, his father's sister, would appear like a breeze and vanish. It was no surprise, then, that as a child he thought she had a pair of wings concealed beneath her green sweater, and that whenever she felt like it, she could unfurl them and take off in flight. She belonged to his most hidden dreams. As soon as the shutters were closed at night, he would open the gates of dreams and secretly let her in.

Of course his mother had contempt for her, calling her "a woman of the world." At an early age Aunt Franzi had left home with some of her friends, and ever since then the reversals of fortune and scandals had never ceased.

She had been a nightclub singer and occasionally a dancer. She had wandered across Europe with all sorts of troupes. She had married, divorced, and been involved in untold scandals, but for some reason she had never converted. In fact, at every opportunity she would declare herself Jewish. She had even composed a provocative ditty that she sang in bars:

> *I'm a Jew and not so pretty.*
> *Before you kiss me, you ought to know,*
> *I come from the fires of hell*
> *And live in Satan's glow.*

That was Aunt Franzi. Some people feared her, repelled by the scandals, but for the most part she was admired. Whenever she appeared, his parents sent Karl out of the house. Perhaps this was another reason he remembered her so fondly.

After years of adventurous wandering, she bought a little house for herself in a remote village and rarely left its confines. The villagers didn't like her, and few of her friends came to visit. Had she converted, perhaps the priest would have helped her, and the hoodlums wouldn't have tormented her. But she refused. The local physician, who was half-Jewish, tended to her when she was sick.

In time, all mention of her faded from the house. Karl's mother fell ill, and he concentrated on his career. Sometimes at night a crack would open in the veil of silence and Aunt Franzi's face would rise up like a spirit. It was said that Prince von Haben, a relative of the Kaiser's, had been infatuated with her and would send her presents everywhere she went. But because of her beauty, people didn't take her seriously as an actress, which apparently hurt her deeply. On the stage she may not have reached great heights, but she was brilliant as a cabaret singer. Peo-

ple would travel great distances to see her performances. Why, then, had she withdrawn from life and the stage? There were differences of opinion about that. Some said she was tired of luxuries and sought simplicity. Others, her detractors, called her capricious. As for the power of her charms, there was total agreement. Young and old were smitten with her, and when she decided to retire, people in Neufeld wrung their hands, as if they had heard she was about to die.

Karl's father was secretly very proud of her and regretted that she lived so far away. More than once he had intended to go to her, but his mother said, "Oh no you don't," and he obeyed her. Sometimes Karl would find her name in municipal files. One of these came his way with the following label: "The Adventures, Betrayals, and Villainies of Franzi Hübner." The file passed from department to department, the clerks adding vulgar comments as it circulated. He had wanted to destroy the file, but the bureaucrat in him was too scrupulous.

After his father's death, he had wanted to bring her some money, but he kept putting off the journey. Meanwhile, his visits to Father Merser had begun. And after the conversion, he saw himself as cut off from his former life, and imagined that henceforth he would have to build a new one. To some extent he tried to do that, but now the telegram had come and struck him from the depths: "Franzi Hübner has passed away. The funeral will leave from her home at twelve o'clock."

At five in the morning, with the last darkness, he left the house. At first, he headed for the office. Then, immediately realizing his error, he turned right and coasted down the slope. Below, the fog streamed densely. Only the church steeple floated up out of the darkness.

By five-thirty he was at the station. The customs sheds were still locked, the cashiers' windows shuttered. On a bench a vagabond slept on his back. Karl stared at the man as if he were a creature from out of his nightmares.

Meanwhile, the train appeared. It was a small train, loaded with coal, and only the last car was meant for passengers. The farmers must have gotten on during the night. The carriage reeked of the earth and pipe tobacco. "To Brauntier," he said to the conductor, glad the name had emerged from his mouth with the correct pronunciation. The peasants smiled the way they do when they hear the name of a remote place.

Only now, enveloped in smoke, did he see Aunt Franzi as he had not for many years: sitting in an armchair, cigarette in hand, her large head covered with curly hair. She always brought him presents from her wanderings, wooden blocks or dolls, and once she had brought him a company of toy soldiers, packed in a large wooden crate. "Here, Karl," she had said. "These soldiers are at your command. Now go and conquer the world." For many years—even while at the gymnasium—he and Martin would play with them on the floor. The splendid regiment in imperial uniform inspired the two of them with something that was apparently embodied in Aunt Franzi: the desire to rise to great heights.

After her first divorce she arrived with a wagon full of furniture and valuables and said, "This is for you, children." There were carved chairs, chests of drawers, treasures from the Orient—everything she had collected or received as gifts from lovers and admirers. Of course, Karl's mother refused to allow these treasures into the house. For several weeks they lay in a dark storeroom. Finally, his father sold them to a furniture dealer for a pittance. He never forgave his wife for that refusal, and every time they fought, he would speak of it as a crime.

Standing for so long in the crowded train erased visions of the past. Karl tried to make his way to the door, in which a panel was open.

"What's your hurry?" one of the peasants asked.

"I need a breath of air."

"Oh. If a person needs a breath of air, that's another matter. But wait a minute. What's the matter with this air? It's not good enough for you?"

"I just need a little more," Karl spoke softly.

"You'd better forget the comforts of the city. Here everything stinks of manure, you understand?"

Karl stared at him without answering.

"Do you understand?" repeated the peasant, adding provocatively, "If you don't understand, I'll explain it to you."

"Explain it to your wife," Karl said, losing patience.

Sensing the firmness in Karl's voice, the peasant's impudent face dropped.

When Karl was a child, the Christian boys would beat him up on the way to school. Until third grade, Gloria used to walk with him. But at the end of that year, his mother decided he should walk alone. Karl was frightened, but decided not to show it. Sensing his fear, the Christian boys would throw stones at him. Once or twice he complained. Then he decided to keep it to himself. The wish to grab one of these fellows and pound his rude face now throbbed in his arms. He wanted them to see what the Jews do to someone who picks on them. But the peasant who had quarreled with him had retreated and fallen into conversation.

In their youth, neither he nor Martin had ever hidden their Jewishness. More than once they had struck those who had bullied them and said, "Jews also know how to punch." When had they become so self-effacing? He couldn't remember. It had been a gradual retreat. Now he felt that if he had only managed to visit Aunt Franzi, his life would have been different. She wasn't what you would have called religious. Her knowledge of Jewish history was slim, but the tribe was dear to her. When she spoke about her women friends or about her fellow Jews, her eyes lit up. Her love for her tribe was a fierce love, quirky perhaps, but constant. She had changed her lovers like dresses, but her love for her people was solid and unwavering. If anyone spoke ill of the Jews or made accusations against them, she would immediately rise up like a mighty fortress.

Among her lovers had been princes, bankers, and manufacturers, but not apostates. She despised them. She would say, "I consider apostates dead. I was born a Jew, and I'll die a Jew." Karl's mother, of course, would mock these oaths and call her "unstable."

The train passed harvested fields, woods, and cattle pens. Peasants weighed down with bundles and boxes got on at the stations. One peasant shoved in a cage full of chickens. The crowding was intense, but no one complained. Some people sang, others chatted. Whoever had nothing to say, pinched a woman's behind. The women slapped the pinchers in the face with great pleasure.

Finally, after five hours of jostling, he squeezed out at an empty rural station that looked like nothing more than an abandoned farmyard. For a moment he leaned against the fence, dizzy from the shock of fresh air striking his face.

The train pulled away, and a frozen silence spread from horizon to horizon. He was in a smooth plain, created not in a fever of heat but with a surveyor's straightedge. Here and there a spotted cow or a black horse, daubs of color in a sea of gray.

"Where from and where to?" a peasant said, popping up out of the silence.

"To Franzi Hübner's house."

"A strange name, a city name."

"True, she settled here just ten years ago. And yesterday she passed away."

"May God keep us from harm," said the peasant, crossing himself.

"Hadn't you heard?"

"No."

"Where's the village?"

"This is it."

"Where are the houses?"

"If you take this road, sir, you'll get to the grocery store. There are always people in there."

"Is it far?"

"An hour, if you're not lazy."

He set out, the bright noon light flowing over the fields. Here and there a puddle glistened. Otherwise, there were no obstacles. For a moment it seemed this dirt road would lead only to another dirt road, and so on, to a dead end. But he saw no point in going back either. With every step he had a mounting sense of isolation—a feeling that since the fields had been harvested, not a living soul had been there, only the wind and the sun. While lost in the cataracts of light, he noticed a small wooden structure nearby. And he heard himself speak a strange sentence: "One cannot know what happiness awaits him upon the earth."

It was apparently a Jewish grocery store, of the rustic type. Noticing the approaching stranger, the owner and his wife came out and stood in the doorway.

"Good morning," Karl called out in his parents' voice.

"A good and blessed morning," they answered together.

"Where from and where to?" asked the husband.

"I came to see Franzi Hübner," he said, immediately regretting his words.

Hearing them, both the husband and wife bowed their heads.

"I heard about it. When does the *levaye* begin?" he asked, glad he had remembered the Yiddish word for funeral.

"She was a wonderful woman," said the wife.

"Everyone is busy with his own affairs. That's a sin that cannot be atoned," the words rolled out of his mouth unnaturally.

"Are you a relative, if I may ask?" She addressed him formally.

"I'm her nephew. My father was the eldest. He also passed away."

"And so it goes," the woman said, releasing a deep sigh.

"When is the funeral?"

"The burial society has just arrived. They're eating breakfast."

"I'll wait for them," he said.

"You've come a long way," she said in a motherly voice. "I'll make you some coffee."

"Thank you."

"Where are you from?" asked the husband, approaching him with a soft step.

"Neufeld."

"I was there once, a very pleasant city. How many Jews live there?"

"Not many."

"We're stuck in this swamp."

"But the view is nice, isn't it?"

"Farm animals and grain make you stupid in the end."

Meanwhile, the woman brought in a wooden tray with a cup of coffee and two slices of black bread spread with butter. Her husband brought out a chair and said, "Sit."

The two of them stood at his side, looking at him with wonder.

Karl sipped the coffee and said, "It's excellent."

"There's more, if you wish."

The sun hung in the middle of the sky, and no one seemed in a hurry. A broad wagon harnessed to two sturdy horses stood in the courtyard. The animals were clearly enjoying the oats and their repose. Karl raised his eyes. The couple standing at his side seemed younger than his parents, yet they were very similar to them. All of their tense being expressed willingness to help.

"Did you know Franzi?" The sound of his voice startled them.

"Of course. We knew her well. She would come here every week to buy food. In the winter she would stay with us. The storms here are terrible. She was a woman with broad horizons. It's too bad she was imprisoned here. We liked her very much, but we always told her, 'You've got to go. This is no place for you.' She was a Jew in her heart and in her soul. In the last year she was very sick and didn't leave the house—just like we are chained to this store from morning to night. We barely make a living."

"I've wanted to come here for so long," he blurted.

"This isn't such a wonderful place, as you can see."

The afternoon light was moderate and pleasant. Now he could see the inside of the store, the sacks of salt and sugar, their tops folded over, and the green wooden cash box. Salt fish peeped out of a short barrel. Their skin transparent, they lay on their sides, looking as if they were frozen in sleep. The smell of corn filled the air. For a moment Karl deluded himself into thinking that he had fulfilled his duty. He had arrived, been fed, and now it was time to go.

"Thank you," he said.

"Don't thank us," the woman chided him gently.

Suddenly, three men and a woman appeared. Karl rose, leaving the tray on his seat. Dressed in linen, they seemed like laborers. At the sight of the stranger a knowing look flickered in their eyes.

"My name is Karl Hübner. I'm Franzi Hübner's nephew," he said, introducing himself.

Hearing his words, the men bowed their heads, and the woman stared fixedly at him.

"We're the burial society," one of them announced with restraint.

"Thank you," said Karl awkwardly.

"It is far to come, but doing a mitzvah is its own reward," said one of them, smiling.

"I'll pay you," said Karl foolishly.

"It's hard to gather ten Jews for prayer, but we managed, thank God," said the man, ignoring Karl's offer.

Every word he spoke jolted Karl's body, as if they revealed his deepest flaws.

"I'm going to harness the horses," the man said roughly.

"Are you joining us?" For some reason Karl turned to the owner of the store and his wife.

The woman looked at her husband before turning to Karl and saying, "I wish we could, but this shop is all we have, and there's no one to take our place. Everything is wide open here. Franzi will forgive us."

"Pardon me," said Karl, regretting that he had embarrassed them.

"If things were otherwise we would certainly go to the funeral, but what can we do? They've already robbed us twice."

Meanwhile, the horses were harnessed and the men climbed onto the wagon with the spryness of youth. The woman joined them.

"I must hurry," said Karl. "Sorry for the trouble. How much do I owe you?"

"Perish the thought, sir. We have enough, thank God, to offer a guest," the man answered firmly.

The wagon was wide, with two benches along the sides and a stretcher in the middle, covered by an old blanket.

"Where are you from?" the woman asked.

"From Neufeld."

"I hear everyone's converting there. Is that true?"

"Not everyone," Karl replied, trembling in his seat.

"They have no shame. I would be ashamed."

What's the fuss, madam? Let everyone do as he wishes. If someone's more comfortable in the church, why judge him? He wanted to answer.

The woman continued. "I don't understand what they find in the church. I'd rather scrub floors than change my religion. Some respect they show an ancient faith." She spoke poor German, mixed with Yiddish, and her face showed the raw anger of someone who's been cheated.

Karl hung his head and said nothing.

"Jews can be despicable too. Don't you agree?" She was relentless.

"I don't know what to tell you," said Karl hesitantly.

"The Jews are strange, a people without integrity or self-respect. They'll sell their souls to Satan without giving it a thought. Even an Austrian peasant wouldn't do that."

The man sitting at her side opened his mouth and in an old Jewish tone said, "Don't judge your fellow until you stand in his place."

"I don't like Jewish toadies," she persisted.

"Why do you call them 'toadies'?" asked the man at her side.

"Because they grovel; they imitate everything like apes. What do they find in the church?"

"Don't speak that way," said the man beside her. Apparently she didn't realize what the three men had already understood, that Karl was among the converted.

"It's hard to keep still."

"I would keep silent, nevertheless," said the man sharply, and with this the woman seemed to catch on.

They drove slowly, the driver going easy on the horses. Meanwhile, Karl's memory, which had been frozen, began to thaw a little. He remembered that he had been tossed about for many hours on the way—first in the train packed with coarse peasants and now in this old wagon.

The woman didn't utter another word, her face seeming to shrivel up. But the man sitting at her side began to speak, as if to distract him, about the rains that had destroyed the summer crops and about the prices that had soared. Karl sat and listened without understanding the muddle of words, which somehow entangled him in their net.

The words brought his parents' narrow grocery store back to life before his eyes. Only on bright summer days would a little light filter in, banishing the musty smell and brightening the shelves. That trace of light was one of the secret joys of his childhood. Sometimes a ray of light fell on his mother's face, and the wrinkles around her eyes eased. Only then would a smile rise to her lips. His father always had a haunted look. Were it not for the few hours he immersed himself in chess, almost like a child, his life would have been worn away in worry and fear.

The wagon stopped opposite a square little peasant hut with two windows staring out like tired eyes. The roof was made of wooden planks, with no gutters, and the chimney was too long and narrow, as if plucked from elsewhere. The door was open.

The dead woman was laid out on the floor, covered with a yellow sheet. At her head were two burning candles. A few Jews sat on a bench and prayed. The candles lit the darkness and the faces of those sitting. Karl was glad he had brought a hat with him. It was a white summer cap, the kind you buy on the banks of the Danube or from the men who rent out boats. The cap didn't suit the moment, but he was glad not to be bareheaded.

The sounds of prayer gradually diminished, and just one broad-shouldered man, with a splendid beard, the kind of Jew no longer found in the cities, prayed softly, as if trying to explain something difficult to his brothers in mourning.

Then the woman appeared with two buckets of water, calling, "Everyone out." The men rose and left. Outside they seemed taller, different from the Jews who used to buy from his parents. Gloom was spread over their long faces.

"When did she pass away?" Karl asked of one of those standing.

"Near nightfall. My wife was at her side."

"Did she die peacefully?" he continued.

The man bowed his head, a smile creasing his lips. Karl realized he had asked a foolish question and was ashamed. Still, his tongue moved again. "How did you know my address?"

"We knew your parents very well. We are from the same place, Bukovina."

"From Zadova?" Karl remembered.

"Yes, yes. Your father and I went to *cheyder* together, and then to grade school. We were best friends. And how are *you*? We heard you'd gone very far. Too bad your father's passed away. Franzi used to speak of you sometimes. She was proud of you, so we decided to send you a telegram."

"I'm sorry."

"Nothing could be done. The doctor said it would have been a shame to move her to the city."

"And how did she spend her last days?"

"She wanted to light candles on *shabbes*."

Hearing those words, a chill ran through him.

The men began praying again. It was a whispered prayer that lasted several minutes and stopped all at once. Two men entered the hut and prepared the stretcher. The corpse, wrapped in a shroud, was covered with a blanket and placed on the wagon.

Everyone got on, filling the benches. The men opened worn, yellowed prayer books and prayed. They prayed out loud but with restraint. Karl remembered that years before he and his parents had ridden a similar wagon to a village to buy goods. Then too it had been autumn, and the breeze blew in his face. He vividly remembered the scene, as if the years had not intervened.

After traveling slowly for an hour, the wagon stopped at a small cemetery. Hebrew letters showed on every gray and moss-covered stone. The grave was ready. The oldest man in the group looked around and said, "Jews, remember to honor the dead." The body was placed carefully in the grave, and they immediately began shoveling earth onto it. When the grave was filled, they put down their shovels and prayed. Karl didn't understand a word. When he was a boy, a tutor came to their house to read the prayer book with him. There was something frightening about the old man's presence. He came for two years, once a week, and finally he stopped coming, much to Karl's relief.

"Say *Kaddish*," they proposed to him.

"You say it—you know it," he said, approaching the grave, then stepping back.

The old Jew said *Kaddish*, and another one, who looked like the grocer who had greeted Karl upon his arrival, delivered an emotional eulogy. He spoke about her arrival in the village, about her loyalty to the Jews. What she had given and how she had given. In her latter years she had chopped wood with her own hands and brought it to the poor. "No one will forget those kind acts," he concluded, "not in this world and not in the world to come." Karl wanted to embrace these strangers, press them to his heart, but he felt unworthy and did nothing.

Afterward, they stuck a wooden plank in the earth, and the women wept.

"How much do I owe you?" asked Karl foolishly.

"What are you talking about? This is a *mitzvah*."

Karl remembered that word, which he had heard at home from time to time. "Then I'll leave this for the poor, in Aunt Franzi's name." Overcoming his shame, he thrust bills into the old man's trembling hand.

"That's too much." The man recoiled.

"No matter. The poor need it."

They climbed back onto the wagon and sat as before,

with the women in front, but the stretcher was now folded. It was evening already. The look of the harvested fields, empty and gray, had changed. A few patches of darkness spread over the edges and glistened like puddles. Of all that had happened he remembered only the coarse faces of the peasants in the train. The anger that had run through his arms throbbed within him once again, but now it was a different anger. He was angry at himself for not knowing how to control his own actions, for always bringing himself into straits. They stopped near the small railway station. "Thank you," said Karl, shaking the men's hands.

"Where are you going?" one of them asked.

"To Neufeld. I live in Neufeld."

Hearing the name of that city, the woman who had purified the body raised her angry eyes but said nothing.

"May God console you," said the old man.

"You too," Karl said, not knowing what he was saying.

# CHAPTER

## 9

That very week he was informed that the senior appointments committee had unanimously chosen him to be the new municipal secretary. Karl was surprised. He had not expected the process to go so smoothly. As it turned out, Hochhut had indeed sought to block the appointment and had almost succeeded. Fortunately, the deputy mayor was behind Karl, which caused Hochhut to give in.

After work he wanted to celebrate, but he didn't know how. He didn't want to go to Victoria's. Two weeks earlier he had spent an evening there and left depressed. He hadn't seen Martin for a month and realized that he was avoiding him. He thought about visiting Father

Merser to apologize for several absences from prayer. In the end, he entered a café. News of his appointment had spread quickly. The owner greeted him warmly and proposed a toast. Karl knew this reception wasn't altogether sincere. Nevertheless, he was pleased, and he thanked everyone present.

Later, he strolled down Salzburg Boulevard. Intoxicated by the fresh air, he headed for the river, which sparkled in the distance and brought back to him the faces of those who had attended Aunt Franzi's funeral. He thought about how Aunt Franzi, after years of wandering, had returned to her people, who had accepted her without rummaging through her past. For some reason the thought pleased him that evening. "Final rest is necessary to us all," he said to himself, not knowing what he meant, but as he walked on, he began to understand. His mother, in her final hours, had pleaded not to be buried in the new cemetery, which lay outside the city, but in the old one, in town, next to her Aunt Betty, who had died of consumption years before, at the age of thirty-one. Karl's father had ignored that last request, because he thought she was delirious. And so she was buried in the big cemetery, outside of town, among strangers.

On his way home, Karl met Harry Baumann, an affable fellow and his father's old chess partner. He and Karl's father would sit for hours in a narrow little café in the center of town, playing chess until they became drunk with it. Often his mother would lock the store, find him at the café, and announce, "I can't do everything!" Karl's father, ashamed, would pull his face away from the chessboard, stand up, and follow her back to the shop. Quarrels were inevitable, and they were as bitter as wormwood.

"Great to see you," said Harry, hugging Karl.

"I have good news: today I was appointed municipal secretary," Karl revealed to him.

"Congratulations. Too bad your parents aren't alive to celebrate with you. They would have been proud of you. I'm proud of you too. I think of myself as one of the family, don't forget."

"I know."

"For quite a while I've been meaning to see you, but I was afraid you'd forgotten me."

"How could you say such a thing?"

"I'm sorry. It's just that I'm so glad to see you. Your father and I were very close. He was an excellent chess player. These days it's hard to find good players like him. There are plenty of amateurs, but not true players. These amateurs, they make a lot of noise, but they don't know how to play. We spent many hours together. Believe me, they were the loveliest hours of my life. Do you still play?"

"No, I'm afraid not."

Once Baumann had had a well-kept shop in the center of town, a profitable store. But his business had fallen off, and like so many others, he had been forced to sell. Now he looked neglected, perhaps because of the old straw hat he was wearing.

"Don't forget me."

"How could I?"

"These days a person forgets even his own father."

Karl walked over to him, hugged him, and said, "My father respected you a great deal. He used to tell me, 'Harry is a truly superior player. There are few like him.' "

"And now I've no one in the world."

"Where's your son?"

"Don't ask."

"Well, come see me, and get me out from under my heaps of paper."

"It's a blessing not to be abandoned in this world." Baumann sighed mournfully and he was on his way.

As if by magic, the brief contact with Baumann brought to mind Karl's father's face. All those years his father had struggled—with the outside world, with his wife, and with himself. He was distant from his son, as if Karl belonged only to his mother. Karl's mother would accuse his father of playing chess at the expense of the store. This accusation simply fanned the flames of contention, for his father could give as good as he got, sometimes making his voice thunder in a frightening way. He had threatened to leave the house more than once. Upon hearing that threat, Karl's mother would pronounce him as irresponsible as his sister Franzi.

As Karl approached his house, he saw that lights were on inside. He thought he had forgotten to lock the door and expected to find some drunken vagrant sitting in the dining room, drinking from a bottle and smashing vases. An old anger flared within him as he went in to confront the disaster.

But in a moment the riddle was solved: it was Gloria, she and none other.

"Gloria!" He walked toward her. "You startled me."

She blurted out a few broken syllables and fell silent.

"Why did you leave?"

"I was frightened."

"Of what?"

"I don't know."

The more he asked, the more her head sank into her shoulders. She was like an overgrown child who had been caught doing something foolish.

"I'll make you some coffee."

"There's no need," she said, bursting into tears. She wept as she had at Karl's mother's grave and, later, at his father's. Her shoulders trembled; Karl hugged her and said, "Gloria, nothing's changed here. Believe me." Finally she put together a few syllables and told him that since leaving the house, she had been working for a wealthy Austrian family. The other servants picked on her, and the head of the family sent her away every time she appeared in the living room.

"You must come back to us immediately," said Karl, speaking in the plural for some reason.

"I didn't behave right."

"This is your home."

"I shouldn't have run away."

"You loved my parents as no one else did," he said and was glad to have found suitable words.

"I was hasty and made a terrible mistake," she muttered.

He noticed that her face hadn't changed: her high forehead, the thick black hair, and the heavy braid that always hung on the nape of her neck were just as he had remembered them. When she came to them from the village, he was four and she was eighteen. Now it seemed to him that only he had grown older. He brought her a cup of coffee and sat at her side.

"I don't want to be a nuisance," she said, looking into his eyes.

"What are you talking about?"

"You have your life to build," she said, echoing a cliché she had probably learned from Karl's mother.

"Me?"

She seemed to him as she had on the day she arrived in the house. Her hearing had always been weak, and she stuttered. At first, every time she opened her mouth, little Karl would burst into tears. But in time he became used to her voice, so much so that after a while other voices were jarring to him. No wonder. He spent most days with her until he started school. His parents worked in the store until late at night. She would play with him on the floor, under the beds, in the yard. True, when he was in gymnasium, he seemed to lose track of her. He was too immersed in himself. In those years she and his mother formed a close friendship. Now she appeared to him once again as she once was.

"You must return to us. I don't intend to sell the house. It is too precious to us all."

"I didn't behave right." She repeated what she had already said.

"Since you left I haven't done a thing. The dust in these rooms comes up to your knees."

Gloria bent her head, like peasants when they come to the priest for a reprimand. Frightened by the submissiveness of her expression, he said simply, "I have good news. Today I was appointed municipal secretary."

"Thank the Lord. It's too bad your parents are no longer living. They had been looking forward to that for years."

"I was informed today."

"That's very, very important," she said, speaking as his parents would have.

Now he knew, if there was any remnant of his parents in this world, it was embodied in Gloria's voice. She had absorbed their lives fully, while he was merely a drifter in their world. His gymnasium years only raised the barrier between him and them. Later came the arrogance and disdain.

The next day he helped her bring over her few belongings. Her employer didn't ask why she was leaving. He just riveted her with an angry glance and shut the door.

"That's no way to behave," Karl called out to the employer.

"Who?"

"You."

On the way home he told her about his Aunt Franzi's death. Hearing the news, she stopped and said, "She too has gone to her eternal rest. She was as lovely as a flower."

They turned onto Salzburg Boulevard, and Karl wanted to reveal his conversion to her, but he didn't know how. Suddenly, the whole thing seemed dark and complicated to him, as if it belonged to another period of his life. Finally, he told her more about his appointment, about Hochhut's opposition and the deputy mayor's support.

Gloria said, "I'm so pleased," and the face so familiar to him from times past returned.

# CHAPTER

## 10

$G$loria worked diligently, and the house, which had known many days of gloom and neglect, seemed to shed its gray mantle. It was the same house, illuminated by the same windows, but somehow different.

"What are you doing?" he asked Gloria, the way you ask a magician about his tricks.

"I'm tidying."

When he returned in the evening, the table was set and the aroma was pleasant. There was always a little surprise: like two flowers in a vase. Now he remembered with exactness her arrival at the house. It was winter. The stove in the dining room was lit, and tendrils of frost twirled on the wide windows. His mother hadn't gone to the store because she had fired the housemaid. Karl was sitting on the floor, playing with big blocks that Aunt Franzi had brought him.

His mother was not content at home, and she expressed her dissatisfaction in abrupt gestures. Karl missed the outdoors. All summer long he had run about the yard, building hiding places, watching the slow movements of a horse for hours as it grazed on the other side of the fence. Suddenly, as if out of the darkness, a short, swarthy creature had appeared, trembling with cold. It was Gloria. Karl's mother had found her near the grocery store. A country smell wafted up from the bulky clothes that covered only half her body. She was wearing peasant sandals without socks, and her knees were exposed and nearly blue.

"What's your name?" asked Karl's mother.

"My name is Gloria."

"And where are you from?"

"From a village."

"Which village?"

"From Schenetz."

"How many years of school do you have?"

"Four."

"And why did you run away from home?"

"I didn't run away. They sent me to work."

"You won't steal?"

"No."

That was the end of the interview.

The next day Karl's mother was back in the store, and he was with Gloria. She spoke broken German in a loud, strange voice. Not only was her pronunciation strange, her whole presence was unique. Unlike the earlier house-maids, she sat on the floor, crossed her legs, and played with him. After lunch she would tell him about her village, which rose up in his mind like a great green castle. Karl had not yet been out of the city.

Gloria was his partner in play from morning to night. When his parents returned from the store, she would serve them a hot meal and withdraw to her little room. His parents were up to their necks in their business. The shop wasn't profitable. Its gloom darkened the house, and every evening they bent over the account books and quar-reled. Karl would play on the floor and, abandoned, tum-ble into sleep. When he awoke in the morning, his parents were already gone. Gloria would say, "Good morning, Karl," and her voice had a pleasant, guttural sound. For breakfast she would prepare hot chocolate and two slices of bread. Her fingers were long, and he liked to look at them as she spread the butter. Later, they would sit on the floor for hours, playing jacks, cards, or whatever they chanced to play. Gloria would say that in the summer it would be warm and green again and they would stroll along Salzburg Boulevard as far as the river.

Sometimes, to make him happy, she would dress him in his new suit, his high shoes, and the coat with the fur collar. Then they would go out to visit his parents. On the way she would show him the wonders of winter: crows and squirrels. His parents were anxious in the store, too. "Where are you going?" his mother would ask with frightening inattentiveness.

Together they amused themselves on the grass in the parks and along the river. After hours of running around and laughter, he would tumble into her lap and fall asleep. One morning Gloria found a rabbit in the yard. The animal was frightened and tried to escape. Its efforts were in vain. That very morning Gloria built a cage for it, and Karl's joy was boundless.

His mother would say, "You're starting school next year. You're getting too old for these games. Gloria, you must teach him to count." These words sounded like threats to him, and he began to imagine school like the monastery at the end of the road, a place whose iron gate seldom opened. When it did, two tall priests would come out and stand in the entrance for a moment. In their dark robes, they looked to him like escaped prisoners.

His father was immersed in himself and paid no attention to Karl. After dinner he would stare at the chessboard, trying to find solutions. Karl's mother would say, "You're wasting your time on nothing."

"What?" his father would answer, as if in a daze.

"Why don't you go to night school? You can get a job only if you have a diploma. The store is about to collapse."

Even those nagging sentences did not pull him away from the chessboard.

"Are you listening to me?"

"What?"

"I'm talking to you."

Those were their customary conversations. Karl remembered them well because they were repeated every evening.

But the morning at Gloria's side was always full of light. She had what his parents lacked—joyfulness. Everything made her happy—a bird, a flower. Even a slice of bread and butter made her smile. During that long enchanted summer he learned to skip rope, play jacks, and fly kites. The kites didn't go very high, but their flight, low as it was, amused him to tears.

During the first years of grade school, classes ended at one o'clock. Gloria would be there to pick him up, and they would stroll along the river, lingering near the fishermen and the boatmen. But the enchanted kingdom remained the backyard, where he and Gloria rolled on the grass, flew kites, and put leaves in the rabbit's mouth. His parents, when they came home from the store at night, looked strange, alien. The question repeated every night, "How are you, Karl?" only embarrassed him.

Gymnasium took him from the house and from Gloria. Neufeld didn't seem like home to him anymore. It had become a jumping-off point, from which he would soar into the world. The house was cramped and limited, and he intended to abandon it, but it soon became clear to him that without money, university was out of the question. Martin's and Freddy's parents had saved money in the municipal savings fund. Meanwhile, Karl's mother could do nothing but wring her hands in self-reproach. It was simply too hard a blow for her to bear.

After the summer vacation, Martin and Freddy left for Vienna, and he became more and more immersed in beginning a career. He made a daily visit to the Green Eagle and a weekly one to Victoria's. The girls knew him well and were fond of him. Whenever he showed up, they would vie with each other for him.

In that deadening routine, everyone was lost to him, including Gloria.

Now it took him time to absorb her return. When finally it sank in, he called out in a voice not his own, "Gloria."

"What?"

"I'm glad you came back to us."

What would be now he didn't know. His recent life had seemed to him like a wave that would one day fling him onto another shore. What he would find there he couldn't imagine.

One evening, after dinner, he said, "I want to tell you something."

Gloria, on her way to the kitchen, froze.

"I don't know whether or not I told you that I converted."

"No."

"I have converted."

Gloria opened her eyes in disbelief.

"Father Merser conducted the ceremony."

"Were there many people?" she asked for some reason.

"All my friends."

"I knew that something had happened," she said, covering her mouth with her right hand.

"Without the conversion, my appointment would have been impossible."

"What can you do?" she said with a Jewish lilt.

"Everybody's doing it, it seems."

"That's true," said Gloria, turning toward the kitchen.

"I know that Aunt Franzi would have condemned me, but you won't."

Gloria laughed and said, "You're the same old Karl to me."

Her comment pleased him very much, and he went over and kissed her on the forehead.

C H A P T E R

II

From then on the days moved along at a different pace. Karl moved into the well-furnished municipal secretary's office. He had known that office since his youth. While still a trainee he delivered mail there, as he did for all the departments. The municipal secretary at that time looked like a replica of the Kaiser, with the same beard and eyebrows.

His new office seemed suffused by a special light, by a special sense of ease. Never, not even in his dreams, had he imagined he would one day occupy this spacious office. Even as the senior committee discussed his appointment, he had not envisioned that this office might really be his. When it was finally given to him, with all due ceremony, he was not especially proud, or even joyful. In fact, he mainly felt self-conscious. The gestures that had clung to him over the years, like the slightly bent head whenever people spoke to him, or the covering of his mouth with his right hand, became so much more conspicuous in this roomy place.

Only in the evening, with Gloria, did he feel comfortable. He would tell her about the events of the day, as in the past upon his return from school. Gloria, to his surprise, kept track of his colleagues by name—which one was a friend and which an enemy. She would listen without commenting, and speak only to foster some feeling he wanted her to.

She had perceptions of people that he didn't always understand. This one didn't look you straight in the eye; that one's paces were too long; another one would only go out with his dog. By comparison, the people he encountered on his way seemed of no consequence. Sometimes she would add, "That's what your mother used to say," or "That's what they used to say in the village."

Occasionally he went to the Jewish pastry shop to sit for an hour. The merchants didn't ignore him. On the contrary, they sought his company, and some of them even flattered him. Karl wasn't fazed. At last he enjoyed what had eluded him all those years—their attention. They would close in on him as if in an embrace. Seeing their attentive faces, he would often fall silent. To their credit, the merchants didn't pressure or annoy him. In fact, they went out of their way to put him at ease, regaling him with stories about the villages his parents had come from, and the relatives who remained there. He had heard a lot about those distant relations in his youth. Whenever they could afford it, his parents had sent them bundles of used clothing and sacks of food. The letters they got back were long and written in Yiddish. His mother would read them out loud and weep.

These encounters were not exclusively cordial, however. Sometimes an old man would startle everyone in the place with his raised voice. The merchants would seize the offender and eject him, but sometimes the old fellow wasn't easily quieted or sent on his way. Indeed, there were a few proud old men in the market district who lay in wait for him. Whenever he entered, they would shout, "Apostate! Down with apostates!"

From the pastry shop, he would sometimes head for the Green Eagle, or else to Kirzl's bar. It wasn't easy to sit at Kirzl's. All of the city's wretched gathered there, cursing and vomiting. The bar resembled the dark corridor of an almshouse. Still, a sense of grace hovered over the place. Kirzl's face was flushed like those of nuns working in a field, and when she scolded one of her customers, bitterness spread over her neck and face.

In Victoria's inn one day, he ran into Martin and Freddy, both happily drunk.

"Look who's here!" called Martin, in the voice of old times.

"You too," said Karl, hugging him.

The place was decorated with vulgar posters and the food was tasteless, but their friendship returned, burning brighter from drink to drink. Freddy's withdrawn face opened, and was lit by the hidden wonder of youth.

"How many years have we been coming to Victoria's?"

"By now, twenty."

"More."

"I came here for the first time when I was fourteen," said Freddy, and his boyish joy, which had been hidden in his eyes, was fully revealed. At the gymnasium it had been hard for him to compete with Martin and Karl. Still, he had managed the impossible and, when all was said and done, had earned passing grades. But a feeling of inferiority lingered in his heart. It showed itself in his posture and some of his gestures, especially that movement of his hand that said, "This isn't for me." But that evening at Victoria's, he seemed to stand taller. He spoke of opening a clinic for the needy, because medicine without caring was worse than commerce.

They drank happily but Martin spoke with muffled agitation about the years he had lost. Had it not been for his wives, his business would have prospered more, the branch offices would have grown, and he would be living in Vienna, and not this dark hole called Neufeld. Freddy tried to sweeten his sorrow, but his words were weak, disorganized, and powerless to bind the wound. Yet barriers fell that evening, and there was a moment of closeness.

After midnight, Freddy, still drunk, rose to his feet

and sang in Yiddish. His song astonished the other drunks. At first they laughed and said nothing, but when he refused to stop, they rose to silence him. Freddy didn't care. He stood firm, in the center of the room, and sang louder. Victoria wasn't in the room at the time, and the mood became rowdy. One of the drunks loosened his tongue and shouted, "That's enough, Jew. If you don't shut your mouth, we'll shut it for you." Until that moment, Martin had contained himself. But now he got up, moved to the center of the room, and called out, "Let no man accuse his fellow. God created us all in his own image."

"But not the Jews," came the answer.

Martin raised his fist and shouted, "God commanded us to love one another. 'Love thy neighbor as thyself.' Anyone who refuses to obey that commandment here and now is asking for a punch in the nose."

The drunk ignored Martin's soused warning. He stood and cursed the Jews with a long barrage of profanity. A trace of the lawyer within Martin must have still been on guard, despite the liquor, because he called out, "There are enough witnesses in this room to accuse you of provocation. If you continue, there will be cause for further charges." In response, the drunk obscenely lifted his leg. Karl, who hadn't intervened until then, immediately jumped up, walked over to the drunk, and shoved him down onto a bench shouting, "Shut your mouth if you can't speak to others like a human being. Otherwise, I'll break your neck. Understand?"

"I'm not afraid of Jews," said the drunk in a voice that suddenly sounded quite sober.

Karl slugged him in the face, and that was how the brawl began. Everyone got involved, drunkards, waiters, barmaids, even girls from upstairs. Karl scraped up his hands a bit, but he fought well, swinging and rarely missing his mark.

It took Victoria, who had been summoned meanwhile, to restore order. As after every drunken brawl there, the floor was soaked and full of shattered glass, and everybody was covered with blood and sawdust. It was very late, and Victoria didn't hesitate to tell the waiters to throw everyone out.

That night the old friendship between the three was renewed. For hours they strolled along the boulevard, eventually turning toward the river, whose surface glistened in a thousand little lights.

"You have to teach the goyim a lesson," said Freddy.

"Don't say 'goyim,' say 'drunkards,'" Martin reproached him.

"Why?"

"Because we're goyim too."

"I'm not a goy."

"You're mistaken, my dear fellow. From the moment Father Merser baptized you, you've been what the Jews call a goy."

"I'm not a goy," he insisted. "I'm an apostate."

"Okay. Fine."

"I'm an apostate, not a goy," he repeated.

"But, honestly now, why not a goy?"

"The word disgusts me. By no means do I want to be called a goy. An apostate—yes."

"As you wish."

"I prefer 'apostate.' Why are you laughing?"

His drunkenness wearing off a little, Karl was astounded at the change in Freddy's behavior. He was the same old Freddy, yet somehow different. A certain power showed in his unshaven face.

"Freddy," he said.

"What is it, Karl?"

"I wanted to thank you for what you did this evening. You were very honorable."

"I did my duty," Freddy said in a voice not his own.

"Your song was wonderful. I didn't know you were musical. Have you always liked to sing?"

"My mother used to sing. They're really her songs, not mine. She sang very beautifully. Yiddish is a beautiful language, isn't it? Let everybody know that Yiddish is a beautiful language. One must honor what is beautiful, isn't that so?"

When they reached Freddy's house, he stepped up to the door and pounded it with his fists. When no one answered, Freddy kicked it and shouted, "Open up immediately or I'll break down the door." Flora, who had been sound asleep, called out, disoriented, "Who's there? Who's there?"

"*I'm* there. We beat the daylights out of the goyim."

"What?"

"Didn't you hear me? We beat the daylights out of the goyim. Now do you understand?"

"I was worried. Usually you're home much earlier."

"Foolish woman."

"Where were you?"

"None of your business."

Martin burst out laughing, took Karl's arm, and said, "Freddy delights me this evening. He's truly outdone himself." At this, Karl raised his voice and shouted, "Leave this stinking province, Freddy. Go to the big city where there's life and not degeneracy."

They left Freddy on his doorstep and walked off. For a while, his voice could still be heard, jarring, furious, but gradually it faded.

"Why am I depressed?" Karl asked.

"What are you talking about?" Martin answered, grasping his arm. "You're municipal secretary, the youngest secretary they've ever had here."

"I'm not happy."

"You have to be happy."

"Why are you mocking me?"

"I don't mock my friends. I'm speaking from my experience and faith. The world to come doesn't interest me."

Afterward, Martin spoke lucidly, and at some length, about the need to move on, to go somewhere else, because everything here was corrupt. Karl said nothing. He sank into himself, and only afterward did he speak about his secret desire to break into the municipal building and set it on fire. Martin, growing ever more cautious as he sobered up, silenced him and signaled that the walls have ears.

When they reached his house, Karl was surprised to find Gloria awake and standing at the door. He immediately announced, "We beat the daylights out of the goyim."

"Where?"

"At Victoria's. Martin, Freddy, and I. We smashed their heads."

Gloria leaned over as if to bow and said, "Why don't you two come in? There's a meal ready."

"Thank you," said Martin, "but I'd better get home."

"But Martin," said Karl, holding on to the doorpost, "you have to eat something. You work so hard."

"I have to get home. I have two cases to prepare," he said, starting to walk. His legs didn't carry him far. He stopped and leaned against a tree for a moment. But then he gathered his wits and, to Karl's surprise, walked on, straight, without stumbling.

C H A P T E R

12

The next morning Karl said, "Sorry. That was a wild evening."

"In the village they say, 'Childhood friendship is hardier than the love of women,' " said Gloria.

"Freddy surprised us. He was a different Freddy. Uninhibited."

"A person has to forget himself sometimes."

"Jews usually don't drink."

"That's true. They don't know how to drown their sorrows."

"I drink, but it's hard for me to get drunk."

"It's better that way. A drunk loses his humanity and comes home like a pig."

Karl went to work without running into a single acquaintance. But on both sides of the street, ordinary people greeted him, and he responded with bows. On his desk he found a stack of papers, outgoing mail to be signed and letters that had just arrived. His schedule was full, but he didn't rush to give instructions as he usually did. He sat in his chair, and images from the previous night passed before him, one after the other, like huge paintings.

Now it seemed to him that his parents had died many years ago, and that he and Gloria had been living together for a long time. Gloria had many faces then: young, as if she had just arrived from the village; but sometimes, on days of rest, a hidden thread of his parents stretched across her face. It was as if she were not herself then but a breathing reflection of their lives. "Gloria," he would sometimes awaken and say, to see if his thoughts had deceived him.

But the charm, if that's what it was, was hidden in her silences. She worked for hours in place, and when she rose, usually from the floor, her face was tranquil and pure. Thus did she arrange the logs in the woodshed, and organize the cellar and the closets.

Unnoticed, the High Holy Days came. On Rosh Hashanah she wore a white dress and placed slices of apple and a dish of honey on the table.

"What's this, Gloria?" he asked in surprise.

"It's Rosh Hashanah this evening," she said.

"Are we obliged to observe it?" he asked.

"An apple and honey are always pretty."

When he raised his eyes to look at her, he saw immediately: there was no embarrassment in her face. And it was clear, her early life in the village and her long years in this house had completely merged. Not only had Gloria become one with his parents' lives, but she also knew forgotten details about the lives of his grandparents, his aunts, and his cousins. One evening she revealed to him that his mother had been determined to return to her native village. Had it not been for her illness, she would have.

"Did father agree?"

"He did, but by then it was too late."

On the eve of Yom Kippur, Gloria prepared two memorial candles, which she planned to light in the synagogue, as Karl's mother had done. For some reason she tried to conceal her plan from Karl. Unfortunately, he came home from work early and found her at the door, wrapped in a shawl.

"I'm going to the synagogue to light memorial candles," she blurted.

Astonished, Karl did not know what to say.

"I'll be back soon," she apologized.

"I'll take a walk meanwhile."

"Be careful," she said and slipped out of sight.

He walked until he reached the river and sat on the bank. Now he remembered the many Yom Kippurs he had spent with his father, walking to synagogue, and the synagogue itself. His mother would seclude herself in the women's section from morning to dark, and when she came down, weak and pale, she would hug Karl hard, as if he had been found after a long search. His father was a skeptical person, and his faith, if it could be called that, was a skeptical faith. In the synagogue a smile constantly floated on his face, as if he were witness to what should not be done in a holy place. But he never protested. On the contrary, he seemed to enjoy the contradiction. Karl liked to observe that smile.

After his bar mitzvah, he never again set foot in the synagogue. His father didn't insist on it, and his mother didn't dare request it. Youngsters have more important demands, people would say at the door of the synagogue, and thus the matter was closed. Later it became clear that practically everyone who studied at the local gymnasium would convert when he completed his studies. Only the children of craftsmen followed a different path.

He reflected that Gloria was now sitting at home, clinging to the gloom that had pervaded it every Yom Kippur in his parents' day, and that thought disturbed him. It was as if something of his had been stolen. He had to admit to himself: Gloria's life was lived according to belief. There were things she openly observed, like going outside at the end of the Sabbath, counting the stars, and announcing that the Sabbath was over. Then she would walk to the stove to prepare a cup of coffee.

He liked to sit and observe her actions. In every one

of her gestures he found a hidden meaning that captivated his heart.

Once he said to her, "There's a contradiction here."

"What?" she asked, alarmed.

"Is that what they did in the village?" he asked.

"No," she answered self-consciously, as if realizing a mistake.

"My mother wasn't scrupulous about observance."

"Your mother was a believing woman."

"How is that? She encouraged me to convert."

"Really?"

"It seems to me that she repeatedly asked me to convert. Am I mistaken?"

"I don't know."

It was difficult for her to explain. Maybe because within herself there was no confusion. She was careful to separate meat and milk. If she made a mistake, she would grasp her forehead and say:

"Stupid head, a goy's head."

"I'm a goy too."

"No you're not."

"But I've converted."

"Ah—I'm wrong again."

Later, if he embarrassed her once more, she would say to him, "Excuse me. As your father used to say, I'm an ignoramus."

When he returned home, the table was already set. Gloria was wearing the white dress she had worn on Rosh Hashanah. At first he had thought of asking her how the candle lighting had gone and whom she had met on the way. In the end all he said was, "How was it?" Upon hearing his question, Gloria opened her eyes wide and said, "I lit the candles and they burned nicely. May God let your parents rest in peace. Their life on earth was not easy." Karl was stunned by the straightforwardness of her reply, which rendered him speechless. The dinner Gloria had prepared was like the one traditionally eaten before the fast, and with every bite he sensed that his life was utterly destroyed, but that if he had an anchor in these stormy waters, it was Gloria. After dinner he thanked her, kissed her forehead, and went into his room.

# CHAPTER

## 13

The next morning he woke up on time. Gloria made him a cup of coffee and he took his time over it, so that when he left for the office he was in a rush. For quite a while he walked without noticing the way, but as he approached the center of town, he saw the locked stores and the heavy darkness in the side streets. For a moment he didn't understand, but then he remembered: Yom Kippur. Walking faster, he circled the customs warehouse and slipped down the narrow lane leading to the municipal building. On the way, he was assailed by visions from his youth: the Holy Ark open, and the Torah scrolls, adorned with silver crowns, as if ready to go forth to the worshipers.

The morning in the office passed as usual. Letters awaited his signature, appointments were kept, and, but for one unexpected meeting, he would have left the office at the usual hour.

At about three o'clock, the deputy mayor appeared at his door along with Hochhut the industrialist. Karl was taken aback but immediately regained his composure when the deputy mayor reminded his two colleagues, both recent apostates, that it was Yom Kippur. It was hard to know if he was serious or joking. Hochhut blushed but instantly recovered, saying, Thank God we're done with all that. Those were oppressive days. Life without the High Holy Days is much better."

"In other words, in the future we'll be done with other things as well?" continued the deputy mayor in the same provocative tone.

"Perhaps."

"It's funny—early this morning I saw some Jews walking to synagogue, and I said to myself, had it not been for my grandfather, who converted, I too would be walking with them."

"When did he convert?" asked Hochhut with cold practicality.

"Ages ago, but I still remember him well. He lived with us for many years. A sworn anti-Semite, if I may say so."

"I remember him. He dressed in hunting clothes, if I'm not mistaken," said Karl, covering his mouth with his right hand.

"That's right," the deputy mayor confirmed.

"I'm glad I converted," remarked Hochhut, as if starting the discussion anew. "I did it deliberately and of my own free will. All those observances and rituals weary the soul. I prefer listening to good music. It's crowded in the synagogue, and everybody is sweating."

In response, the deputy mayor raised his right hand in a vague, swirling fashion and said, "I don't remember much, but I do remember Grandpa Heinrich well. He was a sad and slightly ridiculous old fellow. He wore a shabby leather coat and weird riding breeches. He was proud of his military service and claimed that if they conscripted Jews into the army, they would forget their Judaism, and that that would be as good for them as for society."

"There's some truth in that," Hochhut commented.

"So you think so too?" The deputy mayor was surprised.

"The army would certainly improve their appearance."

"True, but it also creates stupid habits."

"In the army you learn order."

"Yes, but military order is mindless order," countered the deputy mayor, chuckling.

Karl noted the Jewish expression in the deputy mayor's face and wanted to laugh. Meanwhile, Hochhut went on obsessively, "I am not the least sentimental about the old tribal nest. It's crawling with bugs, and I hate bugs."

"I intend to travel to the East to meet real Jews," said the deputy mayor to their surprise.

"Real Jews?" Hochhut asked.

"That's what they say, at any rate."

"I," Hochhut announced, "find no beauty in the Jewish way of life. The Jew is a busybody by nature," he declared, his face turning sour.

Karl broke out the cognac, and in this way the strange discussion was brought to an end. Hochhut told of a new factory he was building on the shores of the Danube. Hearing the news, the deputy mayor raised his glass and said, *"Lechayim,* boys, *lechayim."*

"What's the matter with you today, Kurt?" Hochhut was stunned.

"Nothing at all. I just remembered that's what the Jews say. Isn't that what the Jews say when they're celebrating?"

"Kurt, my dear, your memory is bottomless. But don't we say that some things are better forgotten?"

"Why?" asked the deputy mayor mischievously.

"I don't deny that I was once a Jew, but I can find no reason to boast about it."

"It amuses me."

"Why?"

"The Jews amuse me. They've always amused me."

Now Karl noticed their faces. Hochhut's face seemed rounder, flushed, with a bitter twist to his lips. The deputy mayor was merry as if he had finally come out with a joke that he had been trying to tell for years.

The meeting concluded in the doorway of Karl's office. Hochhut walked off as if reprimanded. Karl sat in his empty office and worked till his desk was clear. Then he went out.

The evening lights glowed dense and cold. Again he circled around the center of town, and then took a short-cut that brought him to the lawn that was called the "Green Corner." The smell of freshly mowed grass filled the air. Years ago he had taken a walk with his father and wound up here. Suddenly his father's heart had opened, and he spoke about his life and about Neufeld. He had never spoken so candidly to Karl as he did that evening. Karl, who had never really respected his father, suddenly realized that not only petit-bourgeois commercial thoughts raced about in his father's mind, but also a few thoughts about himself, about his tribe and its fate. Indeed, his father's words astonished him. Among other things, he spoke about his generation's inability to perceive the light in their ancestor's faith, and from this came bitterness and cynicism. When Karl asked him if he had ever considered converting, he replied, "Christianity is a clumsy faith and has always repelled me. But I wouldn't condemn a young man for converting."

Karl remembered how, year by year, skepticism had taken hold of his face, until no Jewish act seemed honest to him anymore. He often said, "The Jews try to outsmart life, but in the end a ruse undoes its inventor." At the time, that skepticism had the sound of false cleverness to Karl. Only later did he discover that his father had sharp insights. But Karl's prejudice was too strong. He was convinced that a man who had never studied Latin and trigonometry could not have true insights.

Darkness fell from on high, and Karl got moving and headed home. Gloria was sitting at the table, her face gathered inward, and a soft shadow hovered over her jaws.

"How are you?" he asked her gently.

"Everything is fine," she said and rose from her seat.

"There was a lot of work in the office. No end to it." He spoke from habit and weariness.

Gloria leaned against the table, her eyes wide open. He saw the weakness fluttering in them.

"Today Hochhut came to my office. You remember him, don't you?"

"Yes," the shadow passed from her face for a moment, and evidence of the fast was visible on her face.

"Forgive me," he said, alarmed.

"Why?"

"You fasted."

"It went easily."

Gloria set the table and served chicken soup. The smell evoked past years and people as if by magic. He looked for the light that kindled those moments but found only bitterness and fatigue. After the meal his father would sit at the table, smoke cigarette after cigarette, his face closed, as if a decree he could not bear had been imposed upon him.

Later, sitting in his room, Karl realized that Gloria was adhering scrupulously to every act of religious observance that his mother had been accustomed to doing, not omitting a thing. The thought frightened him, and for a moment he wanted to go to her and say, "You aren't obliged to observe all the commandments and customs. The dead are separate from us. You mustn't assume their fate." But those words slipped from his mind, and to his surprise he saw again the long corridor of the synagogue, in whose darkness they used to light memorial candles. Once in his youth he had stood at the door of that corridor and the thought occurred to him then that there is no more fitting image for the yearning of the soul than a burning candle.

The autumn nights were dark, and Karl came home early. The evening hours in Gloria's company would pass in the blink of an eye, and not because many things were said. Gloria would serve him a hot meal and sit by his side. She didn't speak much, but if asked a question, she would answer. Mostly, Karl told her the things that bothered him. She never took him lightly, or soothed him with false comfort.

On Saturday night she would take a bottle of cognac from the cupboard. Sitting together, they would sip two or three drinks. She would tell him about her village, about her mother and father, about her eldest sister, who had tormented her. She had planned several times to return there, but finally she hadn't dared. "One day I'll get drunk and go back. If I am sober I'll never do it," she said, chuckling.

"Do you miss your village?"

"No."

"Then why do you want to go back?"

"I am obliged to."

Obliged by whom, he wanted to say. But he did not. He knew the boundary. To go beyond it would only embarrass her.

The hours in Gloria's company became more pleasant from evening to evening, flooding him with tranquility. Sometimes he imagined that one day he and Gloria would travel together to the country, and that there, far from the gaze of municipal clerks, they would live a simple, rustic life.

"Would you like to live in the country?" he would ask.

"It's not as beautiful as you think."

"But there's tranquility."

"Fear and violence also."

Sometimes on his way home he would stop at the Green Eagle to have a few drinks with Martin. Though it was difficult for Karl to be in his company, still he was pleased. Martin's mood rose and fell erratically. When he was on the upswing, he was enthusiastic, full of wit and charm, and a great companion. But on the downswing— and a fall was usually inevitable after seven or eight drinks

—his expression became narrow and suspicious, as if Karl was not a friend from childhood but a wily customs official trying to entrap him.

At that time Martin had a pretty wife, very independent and an impressive individual. She hated Jews openly and bluntly on account of her first husband, who had been a Jew. Martin would tease her about her prejudices and counter by listing the flaws of the Austrian middle class. Once he went so far as to say they were "rotten to the core." Martin refused to live in her house, and she, likewise, refused to live in his. They would meet in hotels, and their love was furious and hopeless. Martin was, nevertheless, bound to her, or perhaps it would be better to say "captured" by her.

Karl's relationship with Freddy became simpler as the days passed. Poor Jews kept coming to his clinic, even after he converted. Though he wasn't a brilliant diagnostician, his devotion to his patients was boundless. The poor knew it and flocked to him. He too had changed with the years. He had gotten fat and had come to resemble his father, though he was shorter and clumsier. "If I hadn't gotten fat," he confessed once, "I would have left everything and sailed to America." He spoke about his feelings with a touching simplicity. Freddy, who had had trouble with mathematics and Latin, with composition and everything else, was now able to express his emotions in just a few words.

Once he said to Karl, "I feel like a thief."

"Why?"

"I feel that I'm cheating people."

"But you work like a dog and travel to all kinds of remote places," Karl said sympathetically.

"But I haven't succeeded in establishing a free clinic for the poor."

"You already treat all the poor people in the city."

"Yes, but they need a hospital too."

His office was invariably mobbed—by city folk, villagers, alcoholics, the mentally ill. People were always sprawled over his front yard. No one was sent away, and everyone was greeted cordially. And yet none of this did anything for his professional reputation. On the contrary, the rich would have nothing to do with him.

He grew fatter and fatter by the month and dragged himself along heavily. But the words that came out of his mouth were pieces of his soul, as if his girth were some sort of refinery of delicate expression. For hours they would sit in the Green Eagle, talking and falling silent.

Karl would also meet Father Merser, but not often. Sundays had become awkward. It was hard for him to take part in the mass. He would go to church and rush off at the end of the service. Father Merser said nothing, and each time they met he conveyed a new warmth. Once, when Karl told him about his difficulties with prayer, he said, "One mustn't force oneself to pray. Prayer will come on its own." Karl took this as a dispensation and was relieved.

One night, returning from the Green Eagle a bit tipsy, he found Gloria sitting at the table darning socks.

"Why so late?" she asked, moving toward him.

"I was at the Eagle," he said, without hesitation.

"You did well. After a hard day's work a man needs a drink."

"I guess I'm just a creature of habit."

"A drink is allowed," she said and winked mischievously.

He chuckled, and as she laughed with him, he noticed for the first time that her teeth were white and straight, and he had never known her to go to a dentist.

"Why are you staring at me?"

"You have white teeth."

"I do?" she said, as if he had noticed a flaw.

"You have white teeth."

"I brush them before going to sleep."

"So do I, but my teeth are yellow."

"You smoke, my dear."

"Your teeth are so white," he said in a drunken voice.

"You need coffee," she said, changing the subject.

"How do you know?"

"Am I wrong?"

"You are not."

"How strong?"

"As strong as possible."

She immediately went to the stove to make it, meanwhile telling him about her day. The neighbor, Mrs.

Graubach, had gotten up from her sickbed and sat in the garden; the dog stayed by her side and watched over her. "It was good to see her getting some air."

"Does she still remember us?"

"Yes, her memory came back and she remembers everything. I told her about your appointment."

"And what did she say?"

"She wept and said it's too bad your parents couldn't have seen it."

Her few words and the stammer that accompanied them expressed Mrs. Graubach's existence with a kind of precision, and it was clear to him that only in Gloria's language was it possible to talk about the unfortunate woman without arousing false pity.

Her coffee was indeed strong. Every gulp seeped into him and filled him with warmth. The sights of the day gradually vanished from his head, and other pictures, distant but clear, stood before his eyes.

"Gloria," he said.

"What, Karl?" she drew nearer.

"I've been meaning to ask you . . ." The thought took shape in his mind and the words followed.

"Is something wrong?" Attentiveness tensed in her eyes.

He smiled and moved close to her and grasped her shoulders.

"We're old friends, aren't we?"

Gloria looked up at him and chuckled.

"Why are you laughing?"

"I don't know."

"We're old friends, aren't we?" he repeated, as if these were the only words he knew.

Her shoulders shrank as she trembled.

"Gloria," he said, looking directly into her eyes.

Gloria raised her right hand and touched it to her forehead and hair. Karl knew that gesture well and liked it. "What can I do?" she said helplessly.

"Nothing."

"Is there something that you need?" she said, as though waking up.

"No, Gloria. I just wanted to tell you that I'm happy in your company."

"I'm not a young woman anymore." She bowed her head.

He immediately regretted imposing upon her and asked her forgiveness. But he didn't move. He was about to hug her. Gloria seemed to sense the force of his arms and said nothing.

"Excuse me," he repeated. He now saw fear and submission in her face, as well as a glimmer of pride because he had addressed her as a woman. Karl did not look away from her, but he did not know what to say. Nor did his hands come to his assistance. They were frozen.

"Gloria," he said.

"What?"

"Do you love me?"

"My dear," she said, and a smile filled her mouth. "A woman my age no longer dreams of love. I'm forty-nine."

"But you're the only soul I have in the world."

"My dear," she said, and returned immediately to the demeanor of a servant.

"Gloria."

"Not today." She found the words to slip away from his gaze.

"Pardon me," he said, kissing her hand.

# C H A P T E R

## 15

It was a night of ugly dreams. First it seemed that Hochhut was trying to push him out of his office, but then he realized that it wasn't Hochhut but Aunt Franzi who had appeared at the door of his office, dressed in a flimsy nightgown. No longer a young woman, she was still full of vitality and charm. "Not here," he started to say, but she entered anyway and locked the door the way Victoria's girls did. As he drew near her, he remembered her funeral. She laughed the way Gloria did and said to him, "I wanted to fool them. I'm alive and kicking." She removed the nightgown and stood completely naked. "There's a meeting here in ten minutes," he said, the words tangled in his throat. Still, he put out his hand to touch her body—and then he realized that it wasn't flesh but a marble statue presented to him by the staff at city hall when he was appointed municipal secretary. The statue was cold as ice.

The alarm clock shook him out of the dream, and he rose and tried to sneak out of the house. But Gloria, it turned out, had gotten up early and set the table. Her face was no different than on any other morning. A kind of serenity seemed to reside in her. "Thank you," he said, without looking at her.

Only on his way to work did he sense what the night visions had done to him. It was as if they had penetrated the hidden recesses of his soul. He quickened his steps. The first one in the office, he immediately attended to his mail.

Luckily, the morning was extremely busy. Between ten and eleven, when his office was open to the public, he met with Greiber, an elderly merchant who came to complain about his recent tax assessment. Karl spoke with him at length, asking about his son, who had gone to America, and about his daughter, who lived in Vienna.

"You remember all of us." Mr. Greiber was surprised.

"We grew up together, didn't we?"

"Not everyone remembers us, my dear fellow."

Karl could see that the old man was moved.

"Your father and mother were wonderful people. Like you, they helped the needy. A Jewish heart is a merciful heart," said the old man, immediately regretting the words that had left his mouth. He took his head in both hands, like someone who has brought disaster upon himself. "Pardon me, I've spoken out of turn," he murmured with trembling lips. Sensing his distress, Karl got up from his chair and went over to him, "You have nothing to apologize for, Mr. Greiber," he said. "The church hasn't changed us, believe me." Mr. Greiber's eyes shone with relief. When Karl extended his hand, Mr. Greiber drew it to his heart, he was so moved.

Later, Karl attended two tiring meetings—the sort of political intrigues that exhausted him hopelessly. In the evening, he didn't rush home. He sat in the Green Eagle, and with every sip Gloria's years spread out before his eyes. When she was a girl, merchants in the market had tried to seduce her, but she had turned them down, even refusing to have a drink with them. His mother would sometimes say to her, "You've got to find a decent young man to marry. A person has to marry." Gloria would listen without answering or simply shrug her shoulders. Once, a wealthy merchant had fallen in love with her and came to ask for her hand, but she refused him too. Thus the years passed. From her sickbed, Karl's mother would say, "Promise me you'll marry when I'm gone." As she heard those words, tears welled up in Gloria's eyes, and his mother stopped pestering her.

The more he drank, the more such memories were unfurled before his eyes. Gloria as a young girl playing with him in the yard, taking walks with him, and in the evening, his head in her lap as she rode home with him on the tram. Then, Gloria escorting him to school, with sacks of salt and sugar on her shoulder. Thus the images flitted by, and the more he sank into himself, the more he knew what she had been for him, and the angrier he became at himself for exploiting his position, for driving her into a corner. That anger, which had dwelled within him all day long, now spread through his whole body.

"I must ask her forgiveness," he said as he set out.

The light was on in the house. Gloria was sitting at the dining room table, sorting rice. Her body hunched, she was totally absorbed in the task. From a distance she looked like one of the workers he sometimes glimpsed through the windows of a shoe factory.

"Good evening," Gloria said, approaching him.

All the words he had stored up that evening were suddenly lost to him. Instead, he said, "Today the merchant Greiber came to see me."

"I remember him. His store was next to ours. How is he?"

"The inspectors have taxed him unfairly."

"He's a good man, an honest man."

"They pick on the weak," he said, glad that the right words had come to his lips.

As usual, Gloria recounted the events of the day. Mrs. Graubach had gotten out of bed once again, and this time she sat in the garden speaking of her native town in Galicia. Gloria's face was full of wonder. It was clear that this conversation with the neighbor had moved her. For a moment he forgot his irritation with himself, and a kind of autumnal warmth enveloped his body. In his last year of gymnasium Karl had bought himself a leather coat that fit him well and gave him a feeling of height and lightness. He had liked the coat and wore it for years. Two years ago, on a visit to Victoria's, he had lost it. Now the coat returned and stood before his eyes. The sleeves were worn and scuffed, the collar had faded, but still it was pleasant to touch. For a moment he was sure that if only he could wear that coat, all his fears would dissipate, his whole being would immediately be renewed.

He awoke from the reverie, stood, and said, "Pardon me."

"Why are you asking my pardon, my dear?"

"For what I said yesterday."

"We are family. There are no secrets between us." That sentence had evidently been poised on her lips for a while.

"I know, but I shouldn't have said what I said."

"Karl," she insisted, "we're one family. I've been in this house for thirty years now."

"Even more reason for me to have restrained myself."

"No, my dear. We mustn't be so harsh on ourselves. There are things that only we understand."

"I shouldn't have said what I said," he repeated.

"You're as dear to me as your parents were. There. That's what I wanted to tell you."

"But I converted," he blurted out.

"That doesn't matter. To me you're the same Karl," she said, tears flowing from her eyes. She wept like someone who doesn't ask for pity.

"I'll do whatever you want," she added.

"God forbid. You mustn't say that."

"What should I say?"

"You're an honest and faithful woman."

"I only did my duty."

"You did much more than that."

"I don't know what to say."

That was Gloria. How much he loved her, he knew only now. But he didn't know how to express his love. His words were clumsy and embarrassed him greatly.

The next days were overburdened with work. Though it was a strain, he kept his promise to the residents of the city that his office would be open to the public. Citizens came and went, and not only during reception hours. Besides, he was investing most of his energy in the files relating to the commercial center. These were thick, yellowed files in which many injustices had been recorded. It was important to him to cut through the bureaucracy to help people, but the great battle over the center itself was quickly approaching.

Meanwhile, Hochhut insisted on having the center condemned. Twenty small shops were involved, about half of them quite active, the rest in decline. They must all be torn down, he argued, so that a new center can be erected, a modern center, that would comfortably serve all of the citizens. That was all fine, but he was unwilling to compensate those evicted, the old people. What he offered was a joke.

It wasn't difficult to gain support for his plan. At last, a commercial district without Jews. Who could object? Karl felt that this time he could not keep silent, and indeed he led the opposition. The deputy mayor raised an interesting objection: a city without a Jewish quarter, he argued, wasn't a city, and they should preserve what remained of it. Meanwhile, Karl's work routines were disrupted: meetings were now held daily on this matter, sometimes two on the same day.

Karl decided to enlist Freddy. Though his clinic left him no time for other concerns, Freddy's heart was moved by this injustice, and the next day he brought a check for two thousand crowns to Karl's office. When Karl told him that money wasn't the problem so much as public opinion, he replied, "I want to give what I can. I earned this money honestly, and want to contribute it to a fund for the Jews."

So Karl's life changed course. He now spent hours in the center, wandering among the stores, cafés, and kiosks, even entering the synagogue. Those places, which he had ignored for years, seemed less neglected than he had expected. The old men came out to him as if seeking their lost son.

The struggle spread, and numerous parties became involved. Karl, who had spent his entire career in anonymity, calmly preparing documents for the perusal of his superiors, suddenly found himself standing in the political limelight. "Don't call them Jews." he spoke up. "Call them old people, call them weak people—that's what they are, and they need our help." When those words too were ineffective, he went so far as to say, "We converted their children to Christianity, and now we are going to seize the little property they have left?"

Gloria was afraid. She knew that people didn't forgive declarations like that, but she didn't dare say to Karl, "Don't put your job at risk," as his mother would have done. To encourage him, she would open a bottle of cognac, and they would sit and drink. After two or three drinks, her face would shine with a new light. One evening she said to him, "You're a lot like your mother."

There was no lack of scandal-mongers and slanderers in the city. One poster that was pasted on walls said: "Don't call Karl Hübner the Municipal Secretary. Call Him the Defender of the Jews. For Him, the Jews Always Come First." Hochhut was in league with the slanderers, of course. They even mobilized Victoria's inn. Someone dug up an old picture from his gymnasium days: Karl in the embrace of a notorious prostitute.

# CHAPTER

## 16

$A$t first it seemed that justice would prevail, and soon. Following Freddy's lead, several of Karl's friends decided to establish a compensation fund. Justice, in the words of a pamphlet they distributed, demanded that people who had been with us for generations were entitled to decent compensation. To confiscate without reparation was an injustice that would haunt us for years. But Hochhut's insistence on destroying the eyesores ultimately won a greater response. In his distress, Karl sought out Martin, but Martin's mood was very dark. At one point he said to Karl, "I have no feeling for that ugly market. If it's destined to be destroyed, the sooner it happens, the better.

Hochhut was the man of the hour, sought after by every social and political group in town. Even the mayor, who was suspicious of recent converts to Christianity, praised Hochhut. A malicious smugness now shone in his eyes. In every bar and tavern he was toasted and cheered, and his "victory tour" took him to practically every corner of the city.

Meanwhile, the gloom within Karl grew more intense. He felt it in his chest. The collective hostility that had long been repressed in the city emerged from hiding and sank its venomous teeth into him. Everybody shunned Karl, even those who needed him, and his favorite refuges—the Green Eagle and Kirzl's bar—were full of hatred. Everywhere he went, eyes were riveted on him. People spoke of the way "certain individuals" were taking control of key positions, of the spread of bad manners— and now the municipal secretary was even mentioned by name.

The entire city spoke against him. Only by Gloria's side did he feel safe. Gloria had what he lacked, a religious sensibility that knows that not everything can be seen.

He loved her. He could no longer conceal this from himself, but he didn't know how to tell her without humiliating her. His struggles in the office and his path to Gloria seemed to have become intertwined. Sometimes it seemed to him that his rivalry with Hochhut was merely an obstacle to his closeness with Gloria. Sometimes he had the strange feeling that he had converted only because of her. There he was mistaken, of course, for Gloria saw no point to his conversion. On the contrary, she would often say, "You don't have to kneel."

On his way home he stopped off at Kirzl's bar. Despite the hostile looks, he sat with her and had a few drinks. Kirzl also was of the opinion that the center should be destroyed, but she felt that Hochhut should pay compensation. It was shameful to steal like that from old people. She was fond of Karl, though not of the Jews. They were too deceitful. Once she went so far as to say, "The murderers of the Messiah must be punished. How can they be defended?" Only in Gloria's company would he sip one drink too many and say things he didn't dare utter elsewhere.

One evening, when he was blurry with cognac, he said to Gloria, "They hate me. Everyone hates me!"

"You're wrong." She tried to console him.

"No, I'm not," he insisted. Later he spoke angrily about Martin and two other gymnasium friends who had abandoned him. He spoke loudly and coarsely, cursing them both. Gloria was shocked, but instead of speaking she went to the kitchen to make him a hot meal. As he ate, he calmed down. Gloria sat by his side and told him about the events of the day. As always, they were trivial but full of emotion. For a long time they sat together in silence. Then she cleared the dishes and washed them. A youthful smile shimmered on her lips, reminding him of the days when she would bring a sack of salt to the store and unload it onto the shelf.

Karl got up and went to her. For a moment he stood at

her side without uttering a word. Then he said, "Why not be together tonight?" She moved a few inches away, as if she was about to refuse him, but to his surprise she didn't.

"I'm sorry," he said.

She raised her eyes, and he tried to read their expression. A trace of fear flickered in her pupils.

"I love you," he said, immediately regretting the way he spoke these words. Victoria insisted on her clients whispering endearments in her girls' ears. That was part of the ritual,

"I'll go get ready," she said.

He sat in the dining room waiting for her, aware of the sweat that coated his neck and legs. As if to annoy him, visions of Victoria's inn flitted through his mind. For years he had been going there, sometimes every week. The girls were fond of him and gave him more than his due. Still, he would leave depressed. His poor parents were proud of his climb up the ladder of the municipal administration, but they knew that he wasn't really happy. They blamed themselves and their poverty. He had hoped to marry one day and give them pleasure. But time had worked against him.

It almost happened once: the daughter of the district attorney. She was the kind of girl that a Jewish boy from a poor home dreams of—tall, buxom, robust, and seemingly well educated. The romance lasted about six months, but the longer it went on, the wider yawned the chasm between them. At first that distance had a touch of the exotic, but soon he discovered that all the girl cared about was her horses. She kept several at her parents' summer home, and when she spoke of them, her face took on a weird, sensual grin. Her mother was no different.

Their separation was inevitable, and in its wake he threw himself into his work. As for women, he would occasionally return to Victoria's, if only to root from his heart any desire for a prolonged attachment. "A wife is but a tangle of misfortunes," was one of Martin's favorite sayings. Nor did Freddy appear to get any pleasure from his wife. She was ambitious, rude, and utterly without charm.

While lost in these reflections, the door opened to reveal Gloria, dressed in a long nightgown. With her hair still wet, she looked shorter. Her eyes were narrowed as if she had just stepped out of the darkness into bright light.

"Gloria," he said, getting to his feet.

She lowered her head and did not move. All the familiar words were cut out of his mouth. He felt a choking in his throat, as if something shameful had been disclosed.

"Why don't you sit down?" he said.

Surprised by the request, Gloria immediately sat down. From the way her head was bent, it was clear she would do whatever he told her to do, like a maid incapable of disobeying her master.

"You're beautiful," he said.

She raised her head.

"You're very beautiful, Gloria. I'm sorry I never said

that to you before. I'm sorry for all the years that have been lost."

She looked as if she was about to turn her face and burst into tears. He went to her and took her head in his hands. There was no going back. For a moment they looked at each other. Finally, he held her close and brought her to bed.

# C H A P T E R

## 17

The struggle was lost: Hochhut received the approval of the Municipal Council—and its blessings. People celebrated everywhere, from Hochhut's offices to every bar in the city. So great was the joy that a bonfire was lit outside the Green Eagle, presaging what would soon be the fate of the old market.

Karl did not sit idly by. From the corridors of city hall he proclaimed that justice was more important than the market. A modern commercial center built on a foundation of injustice would not endure. Some of his friends tried to dissuade him from making such bold pronouncements. But something within him, stronger than himself, spoke through his mouth.

After work he would go down to the center. He was glad that words like *tsoris, parnosse,* and *reshoyim* were no strangers to him. In truth, there wasn't a Yiddish word that he didn't understand, and if the merchants called Hochhut a *meshumed,* he knew it meant "apostate." Being close to the old men moved him. He felt the freshness of youth returning. The sense of justice, that pure feeling that had once permeated his being, flowered again in him. He was prepared, as he had been then, to stand and prove that life without justice was twisted, and, worse, meaningless.

One evening he managed to convince Martin that the elderly should take precedence over orphans. Ultimately the church would take care of the orphans, but the old people would be left without a roof over their heads. "You're right," Martin said to his surprise. "Why didn't I think of that?" He was drunk that evening and went on about his business affairs. He spoke of them with bitterness, as of a disease that was spreading. Karl walked him home. Near his house Martin promised Karl that he would immediately give the money he always set aside for orphans to the dispossessed elderly merchants. The next morning Karl felt guilty and wrote Martin a long letter apologizing for being so manipulative.

As for Freddy, he immediately announced: "I'll double my contribution. I'm not poor." Freddy's face constantly changed. Every time Karl met him, he saw something dif-

ferent in it. Recently he had seen in Freddy an inexplica-
ble willingness to go wherever life was in danger.

From Freddy he went to Erwin, another old gymnasium friend. Erwin had made a spectacle out of his conversion ceremony years ago when he had declared that the
old faith had passed away and the new one would be sanc-
tified and shine its light upon the world. Some said he
was acting completely cynically, but others claimed that
he had been drawn to the church since childhood. The
truth was not so simple. It seems that Father Merser had
thought it would be lovely if a mother and son converted
together. At first Erwin's mother had agreed, but the day
before the conversion, she changed her mind. In a dream
she saw her mother, who made her swear not to go
through with it. Both Father Merser and Erwin tried to
change her mind but could not. Then Erwin angrily issued
his declaration in the church. The next day his mother
said, "Forgive me for not helping you, but what could I
do? I couldn't fight against Heaven." Later she became
obsessed with fixing up the house. She painted the rooms
and the fence outside, she bought a kitchen cabinet and
new appliances. She also put the garden in order. Her
behavior was a bit strange, but Erwin didn't think much of
it. She had always been subject to fits of orderliness. In his
blindness he believed that this was merely another of
those attacks. One night she took her life with a kitchen
knife.

After his mother's death, Erwin shut himself up in
the house. He stopped going to church, and those who

needed his professional services—he was an accountant—now came to his house.

Erwin approached Karl and embraced him. Erwin's face had changed: his hair had fallen out and his head gleamed from baldness. He resembled not so much his late father but rather his uncle, his mother's brother, who had once had a store in the center and who had died quite young. He and Karl hadn't seen each other for years. Karl never visited him, for reasons he could not explain; and Erwin led a secluded life.

"I've come to ask you something," Karl began rather awkwardly.

"Anything."

"I've come to ask you to agree to help the old people of the market district whom Hochhut is about to evict."

"Gladly," said Erwin. "Just tell me how much."

For a moment they sat in silence. Karl, who wanted to tell him about all the parties conspiring to destroy the center, and about the old people's distress, said nothing. The sight of the familiar house silenced him. Everything was in its place, as if twenty years had not passed. Only Erwin had grown older. Forgotten names arose almost by themselves: Siegfried, Ernst, and Taucher. They too had been baptized by Father Merser, but they hadn't remained in Neufeld. One had gone to the Tyrol, another to distant Leipzig. Erwin spoke, as if for the first time in years. The sentences left his mouth with great emotion.

Finally, he said, "I want to give you two thousand."

"That's too much."

"Relocation costs a fortune. Believe me, it's nothing."

"Others are also contributing."

"But that's what I want to give. That's what I have, and that's what I want to give," he said, pushing the bills into Karl's hand with the same stubborn gesture his mother used to make. Karl now remembered Erwin's mother, who would say, "Do what you want, but I suggest you don't go out now. That's my suggestion, nothing more." This quiet clash of wills would sometimes take place in the winter when Karl and Erwin were about to go skiing.

Erwin walked Karl part of the way home. Outside, his tone turned practical. Speaking of his daily life he said, "My clients aren't many, but they're loyal. I don't need much. I stick to a regular schedule, rising at seven and going to bed early." It seemed to Karl that he was describing the life of a monk in a monastery.

In those days, Karl would return home as if to a secret den. It was a frightening happiness, but happiness nevertheless. Gloria changed. Sometimes she seemed lost in thought. Then a sudden storm would gust into her eyes. The years of celibacy hidden within her had now been turned inside out. Upon his return home he would sometimes find her sitting at the table, doing nothing, sunk in upon herself. "What's the matter, Gloria?" He would rush over to her. The few words she had seemed to have become even fewer. It was hard for her to finish a sentence.

"I'm afraid," she said.

"Of what?"

"What people will say."

"What does that matter?"

"They know everything."

"How do you know?"

"I don't know."

"It just seems that way to you."

He saw that she had covered the bedroom windows with blankets, and that she was about to cover the front windows too.

"That will attract attention," he said.

"What?" she asked, like a person caught doing something foolish.

Her entire life, which had been anchored in the day-to-day, in the order she had created, and in her private dreams, was suddenly overturned. Every noise woke her at night. The self-assurance that had been her charm was gone. It was as if her shame were publicly known. He tried to persuade her that no one knew, that no one could know, and that all that had been and would be was a secret between them. But words didn't help. Still, as she wept, Karl didn't say, "If it distresses you, let's separate." The battles he had fought outside the house had toughened him. He sought to conquer Gloria the way he sought compensation for the elderly. On both fronts he showed the same stubbornness and determination.

It was the height of winter, and rumors deafened the city. The great Hochhut, the all-powerful Hochhut, was in trouble. His enormous project, the sawmills on the banks of the Danube, the pride of Austrian industry, had collapsed under the burden of debt. At first the rumors were dismissed as mad hallucinations, but soon the facts emerged. One after another, the machines fell silent, and the highway that had been choked with trucks was finally empty, without traffic. It was said that Hochhut was trying everything to save his business. Others said that he had fled and that the police were closing in on him.

The merchants in the town center didn't dare rejoice.

A few old men remembered old words—words pulled up from the depths, words of their fathers. Others wrung their hands and refused to believe their eyes. On Saturday many of them gathered in the synagogue. The entire old people's home, borne on canes and wheelchairs, came to pray. Karl stood at the side and watched the procession intently. "It's a miracle, it's a miracle," called out one of the merchants in a loud, vulgar voice, but this was not enough to stop the silent march toward the synagogue. Near the stairs stood two young men who helped the old people climb the steps. And these, it turned out, were Merser's boys, knights of the Order of Saint Gregory, who were sent to help the elderly. They did their work politely and efficiently. Karl stared at them and then turned his back, as he had once done as a boy in biology class when frogs were being dissected.

He could have rejoiced, but he did not. Before his eyes the procession of old people passed, straining their arms to push their wheelchairs. The blind rabbi's face expressed a deep spirituality. When Karl was in the first year of gymnasium, the rabbi had stopped him and asked, "Where are you studying, son?"

"In the gymnasium," Karl had answered arrogantly.

"No teacher for Judaism?" he asked, leaning toward Karl.

"No."

"Too bad," said the rabbi, turning away sharply, as if he had been struck.

The rabbi's two sons, physicians in Berlin, had tried to

bring their father there, but he had refused. The rabbi's house, where only a few years before people took lessons in Bible and Talmud, now stood neglected to the point of ruin. Some drunken thugs who had broken into the rear wing threatened that if the rabbi didn't give them the money he received from his sons, they would set the house on fire. The old rabbi now lived like a prisoner.

Karl remembered the rabbi from the days when he could still see. He would walk through the streets proudly, commanding the Jews not to convert. His injunctions were ignored. Everybody ran after Merser as if he were their savior.

Over the years, the rabbi's eyes had grown dim but not his pride. Often he was seen washing the floor of the synagogue like a janitor. Karl now felt close to that tormented old man, who bore within him an ancient culture that no one wanted. He wanted to approach him and say something consoling. But in the end he realized that words could not diminish his grief. The old man was liable to take it for flattery, or even mockery. It would be better to enter the back door of his house one night, grab the bullies, beat them, and throw them out. That thought breathed new power into his limbs, and he promised himself that one day he would do it.

Later, he headed north and walked along the river for hours. Images of recent days, his childhood friends, and the old people of the center fused into a single vision. It was clear to him that many years earlier a bitter quarrel, perhaps a secret quarrel, had flared up here, leaving its mark on everyone, including himself. But what the quarrel was about, and who it involved, this he didn't know.

In the evening, on his way home, he met Freddy. Freddy looked heavier than usual, and astonishment showed in his frozen eyes. His small cap only made his large, bald head the more prominent.

"We must celebrate," Karl said.

"Celebrate what?" Freddy responded.

"Hochhut's business has collapsed."

"I hadn't heard. I was out in the country. An epidemic of smallpox has been raging there for two weeks."

"In that case, let it be officially known to you that the old center has been saved, and we must rejoice."

"I'm ready," he said like one easily persuaded.

They sat in Kirzl's bar and drank cognac. Karl now liked Freddy's simple company. Not many years before he and Martin used to look down on him, reminding him that he had only passed his tests with the help of tutors. Now Karl noticed: that while his body had gotten fat, his face hadn't been spoiled. From a distance he looked like a merchant, dragging his feet to the door of his shop. His wife Flora had slimmed down to an irritating, boyish thinness. And although at one time she had tried very hard to hide her limited education, in recent years she no longer feared voicing any foolishness that popped into her head. Freddy suffered, but he hadn't the strength to fight back or divorce her. He enveloped himself in layers of fat, to thicken the barrier between them.

Karl looked at him fondly, as if he had rediscovered in his companion a rare conjunction of innocence and devotion. Now he knew for certain that if he fell ill, Freddy would treat him like a brother and would not rest before getting him back on his feet.

"I miss my sister," Freddy revealed that night. Karl remembered Freddy's sister well. She used to run into the house every time he approached. In contrast to her brother, she did excellently in school and had graduated with outstanding grades. But her parents hadn't appreciated her achievement. They refused to send her to the university. Before long, she had married a rich boy who soon squandered his entire inheritance. Finally they were forced to flee to America. Her life abroad had not been easy. At first she wrote Freddy long, detailed letters, but when her parents died, she stopped. Karl remembered her big, round eyes, full of soft wonder. In those years, Jewish girls had no sway over his heart. He was sure they were all bitter and mean.

"I would like to visit her," Freddy confessed.

"You must go soon." Karl spoke with strange assurance.

"My wife won't let me," Freddy said in a recently acquired country accent.

"You mustn't listen to her. There comes a time when a man must say to himself: enough! You've got to find a replacement as soon as possible. There are plenty of doctors. If necessary, we'll get one from Hofstadt."

"Thank you," said Freddy, bowing his head.

"Your sister Frieda is a precious soul, and we must watch over her."

"Fortune hasn't been kind to Frieda."

"You must go to her soon. A visit from you will help her."

"I think you're right."

"You mustn't lose time. Just find a replacement and sail away."

"You always find the right expression: 'just sail away.' That hadn't occurred to me," said Freddy, a smile lighting his face.

"Not always."

"It's hard for me to express myself. I can never find the words. That's always been my weakness."

They parted at nine. Karl wasn't drunk, but his spirits were high. Freddy's company had moved him. He felt sorry for that innocent soul, so much abused by his thin and ambitious wife—as well as by the coarse peasants who woke him at all hours. Lock the door and put a watchdog at the gate, and don't let the peasants drag you out of the house, he wanted to shout, but his throat was blocked for some reason.

"We must see each other more often," he said, embracing his friend.

"Yes, absolutely," said Freddy.

"I'll come and get you."

"Thank you."

"We must see each other more often," Karl repeated, and something of his friend's awkwardness clung to him.

C H A P T E R

19

Hochhut now sought the company of his old school friends, and Karl was one of those he turned to. His arrogance, an arrogance of stone, had been shattered. He stooped at the entrance of Karl's office, like one of the old merchants. Karl tried to ignore him but couldn't. Help me, said Hochhut's sad posture.

Things were worse than people had imagined. Factory after factory, the whole chain of sawmills, had collapsed. Hochhut's house was put up for sale, and the man, once so intimidating, now walked about humiliated and abandoned. A horde of creditors, lawyers, accountants, and brokers all swooped down and seized his properties. In the beginning he had raised his voice and driven them away, but not for long. Disaster followed upon disaster, and soon the creditors took hold of everything. Now of course they reminded him of his Jewishness, and his refusal to finance the renovation of the church.

"What am I to do?" Hochhut stood in the door of Karl's office. For a moment they looked at one another, and a crack opened in the wall that separated them. Hochhut was three years Karl's senior. In gymnasium he had been known not for his learning but for his business acumen. Even then he had run a kiosk near the school gate. In time he expanded it into a buffet. He quickly saw that three hundred hungry mouths are a sure source of income. While everyone else was given over to the whims of youth, his brain swarmed with problems of supply and demand. By the end of the school year, when he was not yet eighteen, he already owned a thriving business. From the start, one business led to another, like a seedling yielding a forest.

Karl had never been in Hochhut's home, but he remembered his parents well. His father was a quiet but friendly man, the owner of a small shop in the center. His mother was tall and ambitious. All her life she had dreamt of big cities, seashores, and elegant hotels, but nothing came of all those daydreams. She remained tied to her home, helping her husband in the store, occasionally surprising her neighbors with some unusual garment. She loved her only son without restraint, and until her last days she spoke of him with extreme admiration.

# THE CONVERSION

Two years after finishing gymnasium, he converted. His parents had hesitated at first, but in the end they joined him. For this they suffered greatly. Their relatives shunned them. When Grandma Hochhut learned of her son's deed, she sat in mourning for him, as if he were dead. His parents bore their shame in silence. Their compensation was their son's successes. His name was known throughout the empire. Hochhut, who stood no more than five foot three, who was bespectacled and bald, was known as the Great Hochhut, the Omnipotent Hochhut.

"I don't know what to do," said Hochhut. "I don't know what to do," he murmured again. When Karl didn't respond, he added, "I'm frightened."

"Of what?" Karl asked.

"All my businesses have collapsed. What am I to do now?" He could barely stand.

"The bankruptcy court judge will seize them. It's no longer your concern. You did what you could. It's no longer your worry."

"Am I to do nothing?" He suddenly smiled.

"The court will take care of it. You need rest."

"And me—what is to become of me?" Hochhut opened his eyes wide.

"You need rest," he repeated.

"Why is everyone cursing me?" he asked.

"There's no shortage of rotten people."

"I'm afraid of them."

"You have nothing to fear. You didn't murder anyone. You tried to develop the area, and indeed you did develop it. You took on a great mission. Very few people take on challenges like that."

"Did I?" he said, chuckling.

"You did great things in the region. Many people will attest to that."

"Then why am I so frightened?" he asked, the laughter frozen on his lips.

Karl understood: the man at his side was no longer Hochhut but what remained of him. Yet Karl still did not trust the man.

"Why am I so frightened?" Hochhut muttered again, his voice trembling. Now he resembled his father when he held his forehead or wrung his hands.

"You need rest. You must sleep. You've had some hard days." Karl tried to approach.

Hochhut didn't move. Karl took his arm, saying, "I'll walk with you. You have nothing to fear."

"They won't attack me?"

"Certainly not."

At first he thought of taking him home, but then he remembered that Hochhut's house had been impounded, so he decided to take him to his own home. But Hochhut refused to cross Hapsburg Boulevard. He claimed that his enemies were hiding in the trees, waiting to ambush him. Karl's promises that no harm would befall him were useless. Hochhut was in the grip of dread.

Eventually, Hochhut went with Karl, but not in the direction of his house. Instead, they headed toward the hospital. Karl tried to distract him, but Hochhut wasn't listening. At the corner of Hapsburg Boulevard and the Poets' Street, Hochhut's old voice returned to him for a moment. He spoke of two serious mistakes he had made in his life. The first was forcing his parents to convert. The second was the premature sale of two forests in the Tyrol.

Later, he spoke of all the enemies ready to ambush him in the Royal Grove. A thin, awful laugh sealed his lips. Not far from the hospital he said to Karl, "I want to tell you a secret. Swear not to tell anyone. Do you promise?"

"You have my word of honor," said Karl.

"I have another little factory in Italy. It's registered in my Aunt Sylvia's name. No one knows about it, and it stands a good chance of expanding. But don't tell a soul, do you promise me?"

"On my word of honor."

"If things turn out right, I can reopen some of the factories that have collapsed. It's not a big operation but it's stable. I can shift the focus over there for a while. Aunt Sylvia doesn't even know there's a factory in her name. You do believe me, don't you?"

"Of course I do."

"My enemies in the Royal Grove must be rounded up immediately. The City Council must issue an order. I have given a great deal to this city. I deserve something in return." For a moment his old face returned, assured and arrogant. He grabbed Karl's arm and said, "You mustn't abandon me. Tell them that I'm under your protection."

Once he was in the hospital he relaxed. He didn't resist. The doctor on duty, Dr. Meisler, his old classmate, knew immediately why he was there and embraced him.

"I knew that one day you'd get me," Hochhut joked. "But no injections. I'm afraid of injections."

"You have nothing to fear. I'm on your side."

"I thank my kind and generous classmate. I thank the whole staff," said Hochhut, bowing.

Karl once again saw that the Great Hochhut, the Omnipotent Hochhut, was no longer among the living. The man who had bowed was merely his shadow, and soon that shadow too would fade.

"Hochhut came to my office today," he said in a dry tone, as if he were standing before the City Council and reporting on a survey of the water system. "I immediately saw that he wasn't well and I decided to bring him here."

"That's absolutely correct," said Hochhut, chuckling.

"It's good that you came here," said Dr. Meisler.

"And now they're going to give me an injection," said Hochhut, twisting his shoulder. "I hate injections."

"No one will do anything to you. Just rest for a while," said the doctor.

"I'm not tired," said Hochhut.

"Yes, you *are* tired." Meisler spoke to him as if he were a child.

"And what will Karl do? I can't leave him. He was a big help to me."

"Karl will visit you. I'm sure he'll come to visit you."

"And I'll stay here?"

"Exactly. You have nothing to worry about. Everyone is very nice here."

When Karl returned home, Gloria saw that his face was different. She quickly served him a hot meal but didn't dare ask him anything. Karl washed his hands and, without saying a word, sat at the table. Later, he told her, in a choked voice, about the state he had found Hochhut in and about their walk to the hospital.

"I never imagined that a strong man, a man who had managed great factories, could be so frightened." Gloria sat close by his side, trying to catch every syllable he uttered. A strong light, a strange light, flickered on Karl's face, and Gloria saw that something of Hochhut's dread had seeped into him.

# CHAPTER

## 20

Hochhut's shadow wouldn't fade from Karl's eyes. On his way home, along Hapsburg Boulevard, he could hear his thin laughter, that frightening trace of Hochhut's mighty presence, filtering through the naked trees. Sometimes it seemed that a bit of that laughter was clinging to him also.

It was difficult to speak about this fear to Gloria. Hochhut's illness had seeped into him. He would see Hochhut getting up from his sickbed and attacking his creditors, but usually he saw him as he had been that afternoon in his office: stooped, helpless, frightened.

Once a week he went to the hospital to ask about

Hochhut. His illness, it appeared, had grown worse, and Meisler no longer allowed Karl to see him. In the silenced sawmills, the bankruptcy receivers walked about unhindered, like lords; and creditors lay in wait on all sides, vultures eager to feast on a carcass.

At night he would have a few drinks with Gloria and tell her about the office. It was hard for him to keep the outside world at bay. The people in the city hadn't forgotten his opposition to the destruction of the old market, and at every opportunity they reminded him of his sin. Karl wasn't afraid. He was prepared once more to stand up and proclaim a scoundrel anyone who stole an old man's livelihood. In her heart Gloria knew that his stubbornness would damage his career, but she was proud of him. He was once again a fearless boy, who would annoy not only his parents but also his adversaries. The nights with Gloria were an intoxicating blend of memory and oblivion, of what had been and of what would be. Were it not for the arrival of morning, it would have been even more extraordinary.

He kept his distance from Martin. It was hard for him to put up with Martin's drunkenness and nasty comments. Karl wanted to reproach him about that, but he couldn't find the strength.

One evening, on his way home, he ran into Martin.

"You've been avoiding me," Martin accused.

"Why do you say that?"

"That's the feeling I have."

"That's nonsense. I have no secret to keep from you."

Later, they sat in the Green Eagle and drank cognac. They spoke Hochhut's fate. Formerly, Martin had been Hochhut's legal advisor, drafting contracts and representing him in court. In time they parted because Hochhut wanted to insert intentionally ambiguous clauses in his contracts, mainly to gain time. His power lay in his manipulation of time.

"He was at war with the principle of time," Karl said, trying to get to the heart of the matter.

"No. He wasn't that philosophical. He was just always exploiting the interval between purchase and sale. That was his genius. I was a young lawyer and for a while I didn't see what he was up to. I'm sure he was deceiving everyone."

"Then what happened?"

"I suppose he lost his sense of timing."

"Is there any hope?"

"It's already too late, I imagine."

"He hated Jews, didn't he?" said Karl, turning up the heat on a different burner.

"They bothered him a lot."

"And he couldn't overcome his hatred."

"It was too deep."

"Once I wanted to scold him for his extreme hostility to the Jews, but he appeared so sure of himself that I started wondering if he wasn't right," Karl admitted.

"Well, he had been talking about modernizing the old center for a long time."

"Without taking the people into account."

"Yes, that's true. He saw the Jews, as long as they remained Jews, as the enemies of humanity."

"Strange."

"Not really. We abandoned them too."

"For different reasons, it seems to me."

"Come, now. Let's face it: we didn't like them. They revolted us."

"That's a very harsh statement."

"But it's true."

"I'm not so sure," Karl disagreed.

"Why, then, did you convert?"

"For my career, to tell you the truth."

"Let me understand this, Karl: You changed your religion because you wanted to rise up the ranks?"

"Correct."

"A person converts for a promotion? I left the Jews because their whole way of thinking—their character and their behavior—disgusted me."

Karl sensed that his friend was somehow trying to trap him. That evening he had no strength to fight. Leave me alone, he wanted to tell Martin. Why torment me? Why poison our friendship? But he couldn't, and Martin kept pounding away: "And what did Father Merser say to you about that?"

He wanted to say that he hadn't told the priest about his secret. Instead he replied, "Father Merser understood me."

"That surprises me."

"He understood me," Karl repeated.

Karl realized that Martin had now trapped him. Fear fell upon him, as in a nightmare.

"I have to get home," Karl said, rising from his chair.

"Too bad. I'd like to talk about this some more," Martin badgered.

When Karl returned home, Gloria knew by his expression that his day had been hard. She served him hot soup and didn't ask a thing.

"Martin was very crude," Karl said without raising his head.

"Yes, I passed him the other day on the street. He looked tense."

"One mustn't speak that way."

"In the village they say: 'Keep away from tense people, the wolf dwells within them.' "

"Tonight he murdered our friendship in cold blood. I should have responded. I'm furious that I didn't."

"What was he talking about?"

"Hochhut, but really he meant me. He was attacking me directly."

"What did he want?"

"I don't know."

After a pause he said, "I didn't convert because I was convinced of Jesus' miraculous birth, but because I realized that without converting they wouldn't appoint me municipal secretary. Is that deceitful?"

"I didn't understand your question," said Gloria.

"I'm asking you if that was deceitful."

"You tell the truth. Your late mother used to say, 'Karl tells the truth, and that won't make his life any easier.' "

"Is that what she said?"

"Yes, that's what she said. On my word of honor."

That night Karl's sleep was dark and deep. He woke up late and didn't reach the office till nine. As soon as he entered, he sensed that something was wrong. He wondered if the janitors had gone on strike again. The department director's door was closed, which increased his suspicion. But when he reached his own office, he was relieved to find everything running smoothly. For a full hour he sat and answered letters. In some of the letters he was asked about Hochhut's plans. His responses were brief and to the point. The gist was: for the moment we must wait. In the afternoon his secretary entered and announced, "Schmidt the lawyer died last night."

"Which Schmidt?" asked Karl.

"Martin Schmidt."

The rock fell down from the mountain.

He rushed out and without thinking headed for the Green Eagle, where he had left Martin the night before. As he stood outside the place, he realized the foolishness of having gone there. Still, he opened the door and peeked in. The place was empty and dark. Karl went back out to the street.

"What's the matter?" he asked himself in his normal voice. He stopped and thought for a moment and then broke into a run in the direction of the hospital. Only once he had come to the Royal Grove did he realize that there was no reason to run.

Dr. Meisler greeted him with a nod. Conversion, Karl realized, had done nothing for the doctor's face. It had become even more Jewish, and now with his beard, he looked just like his father, who had owned a bakery in the old center.

"I sat with Martin last night until nine," Karl told him. "He didn't complain of anything."

"At a quarter to ten he was dead," said the doctor, and a pained smile spread on his face.

"How did it happen?" asked Karl.

"Just like that, my dear fellow. Just like that." The doctor spoke in the manner of an old Jew.

"We quarreled, but in a friendly way," said Karl.

"This didn't happen because of one conversation or another." Meisler absolved him of guilt.

"Aren't there warning signs?"

"There are, but we usually ignore them."

Later, he thought of going to see Freddy, but he lingered in the hospital. From the psychiatric ward, which was housed in a separate building, terrible screams were heard. Several hefty patients stood at the barred windows waving their arms at the passersby. No one went near them. The thought that Hochhut, too, was now among them made Karl's knees buckle momentarily. He started for Meisler's office, then changed his mind and headed off to find Freddy. The maid told him that peasants had awakened him before dawn and he had gone out to the village and not yet returned.

From there he went down to the river. Memories from their gymnasium years were mingled with visions of the past few days. He thought if he hurried he might meet up with Freddy, who would be returning by way of the bridge. The pale winter light hung wearily on the trees, and heavy shadows spread over the ground. The moist air brought to mind the trips along the river that he and Martin used to take together in the winter. Those were days of great excitement, and hunger, and boundless energy.

The next day he and Freddy sat together in the Green Eagle, lost in the crowd.

"He didn't take very good care of himself," said Freddy.

"But he always seemed so strong and self-confident."

"As a physician, I should have warned him."

"He insulted me a lot, but I never said a thing to him," Karl stammered.

Later, Karl spoke angrily about the tragic waste of Martin's life. He blamed Martin's wives for embittering him, and nor did he spare Father Merser, who would pressure Martin whenever he needed a big contribution. In the end he said, strangely, "We need to avenge his death."

The funeral was short and cold. Father Merser, who led the memorial service, spoke of Martin as a Christian whose Christianity had not been inherited but chosen and deliberate. He recalled Martin's generosity, his many contributions to the church and the orphanage. The heavy odor of incense permeated the air, and Karl found it hard to breathe. Most of those attending were attorneys, along with a few of the judges before whom Martin had argued cases. Everyone sat silently. Martin's wives didn't come, not even the one with whom he'd lived in a hotel. No one wept. It was as if everyone had agreed that this is the way one must leave this world. Later, by the grave in the open air, Karl was still having difficulty breathing. A Jewish funeral may be hasty and disorganized, he thought, but it's human. A funeral without weeping is empty and cruel.

As he walked among the mourners, he passed a grove of trees draped in a thin layer of frost. Karl recognized them. They were the tall birches that surrounded the playing field next to the cemetery. On bright, cold autumn days, the shadows of their thin branches would quiver on the ground with the delicacy of a Japanese painting. In their last gymnasium year, he and Martin had played a lot of volleyball. Martin was one of the best. His leaps at the net were precise and elegant. He rarely missed a shot or a block. Now before his eyes, Karl saw those leaps in slow motion.

The president of the Bar Association read a eulogy praising Martin's contribution, speaking especially of the organization's bylaws, which Martin had taken great pains in formulating. Then those in attendance shook hands again and spoke about business and public affairs. Winter was everywhere, and dark clouds moved across the sky.

Meanwhile, Karl remembered that in the second year of gymnasium Martin had written a poem on winter. The teacher, Mrs. Sperber, had praised it and said, "Martin is sensitive to colors and sounds. Let us pray that he doesn't lose that sensitivity." The word "pray" had sounded very strange back then. Now that word seemed to return across the distance of years and glow, like Mrs. Sperber's face, which he had loved to look at.

After the funeral he and Freddy went to Kirzl's. The place was full of drunks, and they could barely find a place to sit. After the first drink, Freddy started to cry and say strange things: "We're so few and so isolated, and now we've lost Martin too. You could always turn to him."

"The work you do is so important." Karl changed the subject.

"It's a drop in the ocean, believe me."

"Everything *I* do is a lie. It's all manipulation and paperwork. I'm fed up with it," Karl groaned.

"Martin's wives really put him through hell. You were smart not to marry."

"What good has it done me?"

Thus they sat and talked and rambled on, like two old men whom the tempest of life had tossed up on a barren shore.

The next day, the anniversary of his father's death, Karl went to the Jewish cemetery. The guard greeted him and handed him a yarmulke. As he stood among the gravestones, the sight of Martin stayed with him. Before every volleyball game, Martin would skip rope to warm up. The agility of his entire being was expressed in those skips.

"How are you?" the guard asked him.

"My friend Martin was suddenly snatched away." He couldn't hold it in.

"I heard. Years ago, when I owned a shop in the center, he would come to me to buy lollipops."

"We were unable to help him." Karl couldn't control his emotions.

"He was always scrupulous about coming on his parents' *Yahrzeit*. Just a month ago he was here. He knew the *Kaddish* by heart."

"I can't understand how we failed to see his distress."

"That's how life is—short and untidy."

The evening lights faded on the trees, and Karl returned to Salzburg Boulevard. He was moved by the warmth of the cemetery guard. An old power, a power he hadn't felt for years, once again throbbed in his arms. It was cold, and he was hurrying home. But a few minutes from the house he suddenly veered off in another direction and soon broke into a run.

In a short time he was standing in the courtyard of the rabbi's house. Immediately he rushed to the back of the house, leaped in through a window, and shouted, "Get out! Everyone in this part of the house must get out!" There was no answer.

"I repeat: Everyone in here must get out! Otherwise I'll throw you out!"

The darkness was absolute, but from his corner he could just make out the squatters sprawled on the floor. The smell of beer mixed with tobacco hung in the room.

"Who's there?" one of them said, getting off his mat.

"Never mind. Just get on your feet and get out."

"This is our house."

"It's not your house. It's the rabbi's house. You're squatting here illegally."

"What rabbi?"

"The Neufeld rabbi."

"We're Christians, if you want to know. What do we care about a rabbi?"

Karl didn't say another word. He leaped over to the man's mattress, grabbed him, and pushed him out. Then he made a bundle of his belongings and threw them out the window. Two others, seeing what Karl had done to their companion, shouted, "Thief!" Karl shoved them out too.

"If anyone dares come back in, he'll regret it. The rabbi is an old man. You are not to disturb him."

"Who are you?" Another of the squatters woke up.

"I'm from the police."

"And you're defending the Jews?"

"We defend all citizens, no matter their religion."

"Since when? Where are we supposed to sleep?"

"Outside, or in the city shelter, but not here. The whole world isn't up for grabs."

"Hey, we're not kids anymore."

"We expect a little respect from adults. And I warn you: I'll personally beat up anyone who threatens the rabbi or extorts money from him."

"We can't stay here?"

"Not anymore." Whoever is found here will get the living daylights beaten out of him. We're going to make an inspection every night."

When he got home, Gloria asked, "What's the matter?"

"Nothing."

After dinner he told her that he had gone to the cemetery to visit his parents' graves. The cemetery was well tended, and the headstones hadn't been damaged. Gloria made no comment and asked no questions. During the summer, before the High Holy Days, she used to visit both Jewish cemeteries of the city, the new one, where Karl's parents were buried, and the old one, where his Aunt Betty's grave was.

The following days were tense and gloomy. Rumors spread throughout the city that Karl and Gloria were secretly living together, and everywhere the matter was discussed with malicious pleasure. Gloria told him that young thugs had chased her in the street and called her a dirty whore. The rumor had not escaped Kirzl's bar, either. A beggar shouted at Karl, "A Jew is always a Jew. You can never trust him." Karl walked up to him, intending to hit him, but seeing that it was a ragged old man with no teeth, he was too disgusted to do him any harm. Anyone in the office who dared say a word was reprimanded and warned that he would be fired.

Fear of Hochhut hadn't left the center. The merchants came to ask Karl's advice, and he advised them to sell out while it was still possible. Nothing could be done. The center was doomed. The news was harsh, but the merchants left his office with their heads held high, as if they had just discovered that the whole world wasn't lawless. One of the old men couldn't restrain himself and said, "We'll remember you, my dear fellow, even in the next world. And we're not far from there now."

The winter ended but Gloria seldom left the house. She stored the winter clothes and took out the spring ones. The smell of naphthalene spread through the house, and with it the feeling of relief. Gloria loved that work and did it diligently. Her youth and her maturity were buried in those closets and cupboards. At one time Karl had wanted to donate the clothes to the old age home, but Gloria stopped him. She knew: the maids there steal everything, and only rags would reach the old people.

After Martin's death something changed in Karl's life. Suddenly, the formalities of the office, to which he had been accustomed for years, seemed pompous to him. The indirect, euphemistic language of bureaucracy also lost its charm. What he had to say now, he said in a simple way that anyone could understand. Martin's face, as if from spite, was always before him. He found it in every corner of the city, in the strangest places. Since Martin's death, his own life had seemed more tangled. But sometimes he felt he was free and had only to decide what he would do next. But what he would do, and how, he didn't know.

Every night he would steal into the rabbi's courtyard, wake the squatters, and hurl them out with their belongings. One night a squatter drew a knife. Karl didn't hesitate. He pounded the man's face with his fists.

The evil spirits did not subside. Every day letters came to the mayor and to the City Council, demanding Karl's dismissal. If before they had complained that he was protecting the Jews of the old market, now they complained about his depravity.

"Hypocrites," Karl responded.

In his practice, Martin had filed some lawsuits against slanderers, and there were some well-known cases in which the victims had received compensation. Now there was not a single lawyer in the city to whom Karl could turn for advice.

At first the other converts were pleased that Karl had converted. But over the years he observed that they seldom showed themselves in public, preferring to lead their lives in seclusion. They were never eager to meet with childhood friends. In the summer they fled to the Tyrolean Mountains, where they blended in with the locals.

He occasionally saw Father Merser, who of course knew about Karl's troubles. His advice was simple: one Sunday soon he would make the pulpit available to Karl, so that he could tell the congregation what had happened and how. The proposal, which sounded, on the face of it, so logical and generous, embarrassed Karl.

"What should I say?" asked Karl.

"Whatever there is to say," answered Father Merser.

He knew: it wouldn't be just a lecture. Insulting questions would follow. He would have to justify himself, speak of personal matters, say something about his new faith. As for Gloria, he would have to mention that she had worked in his home since he was a child. Explain that she was fourteen years older than he.

"It's hard for me to talk about my personal affairs," said Karl.

"As you wish."

Thus he avoided that trap. Meanwhile, Gloria continued to shop in the center. The greengrocers abused her and called her a slut. Sometimes her village tongue would return to her and she would stand fast and curse them like a peasant woman, but mainly she felt herself at a loss and would return home stooped and humiliated. Finally, she shut herself up in the house. After work Karl would buy groceries and return home loaded with shopping baskets.

The attacks intensified and came from all sides, now striking at the house itself. Karl would lie in wait for the attackers and scare them off. Sometimes he would catch one of them. They were mainly the kind of young people from outlying neighborhoods who, after work in a factory and downing a drink or two, would invade the center, jeer at the old men, and steal their money. Recently they had found a new target: Gloria. At first, Gloria gave as good as she got. She cursed them and their mothers. But Karl would not submit, even as the earth was collapsing from under their feet. At the same time, though, he had begun dreaming about a long trip to the provinces. When she heard his plans, Gloria's face would become worried, as if he were speaking of some frightening delusion.

"And after the trip, will we return here?" she would ask.

"No."

"Where will we live?"

"In different cities. Isn't that more interesting?"

"And we won't have a house?"

"Why do we need a house?"

The nights were still quiet, and Karl would sink into Gloria's body with total abandon. In the morning he would get up late and hurry to work.

One evening a gang descended on the house. Without hesitating, Karl went after them. But this time they were quicker than he. One of them threw a knife and struck Gloria's shoulder. When Karl returned, he found Gloria lying flat on the floor.

He summoned Freddy, who came in his carriage. Seeing that the wound was deep, they quickly got her to the hospital.

After Freddy had conferred with the staff doctor about Gloria's wound, Karl spoke excitedly about the need to combat the spread of violence. He sounded like those young Jews who had fled to Russia to learn how to fight injustice. That night Karl and Freddy sat up in the hospital café until very late. Karl told him he was thinking of resigning from his position and going out into the provinces.

"What will you do there?" Freddy asked anxiously.

"I don't know. I need trees now, not people."

"I wouldn't leave a steady job," said Freddy.

"I've had my fill of people. I'm hungry for some trees and streams."

Hearing those words, Freddy opened his eyes wide, as if Karl had said something truly astonishing.

That night Karl felt that everything around him was closing in on him. Rage gnawed at his limbs. Freddy was his only friend left in Neufeld. Still, it was hard to rely on him. His heart was boundless, but his mind could be narrow. Every time he encountered a problem, he would revert to his parents' tired notions. "I wouldn't leave a steady job," he had repeated several times that night. And for some reason he was sure that Gloria had been stabbed because she was involved in a dispute. "Housemaids are always quarreling," he declared.

"Gloria doesn't quarrel. I'm the one who quarrels."

"So why did they stab her?"

"Are you asking me?"

Freddy wasn't about to grasp Karl's relation to Gloria. His opinion was that if Gloria returned to her native village, things would go more easily for Karl.

Why are you so naïve, my dear fellow, Karl wanted to say.

After two weeks, Gloria was released from the hospital. Immediately she began tidying the house. Karl's pleas were of no use: "You've got to rest," he said. "Anyway, we're leaving."

"Where will we go?"

"To the Carpathians. Haven't we said they're a wonder of nature?"

"It's all because of me."

"I need trees now, not people."

"I'm the one who must leave, not you."

"Both of us," he said, smiling.

He put the house up for sale. Agents and buyers would come and go during the evening hours. They were quick to point out the flaws: too close to the old town center, the ceiling was low, the floor was sinking. Karl saw their cunning attempts to depreciate the property. In the end, their offers were barely half the house's value. But what irked him most were not the low offers themselves but the way they were made—in a teasing, mocking manner calculated to insult.

"I won't sell to them," he reported to Gloria without comment.

"As you wish."

She had apparently underestimated his determination. At the end of March he wrote a brief letter to the mayor announcing his intention to resign. The mayor's reply was courteous, but he did not ask him, as was customary, to postpone his decision. Nor did he ask to see him. If that's how it is, Karl said to himself, then I acted correctly.

The house wasn't yet sold. Meanwhile, Gloria cried at night, and Karl promised her that life in the Carpathians would be a life of truth, without pretense or fear.

One evening on his way home he met his friend Erwin.

"I'm leaving for the Carpathians," Karl told him.

"On a trip?"

"Forever."

"You mean you won't be coming back here?"

"I don't think so."

"Strange," said Erwin, and the astonishment in his face grew deeper.

"I'm glad to get free of this prison," said Karl.

"Prison?"

"What else could I call it?"

"In the Middle Ages, they used to call the body a prison, so why not?"

"Don't you feel that the empire is disintegrating?"

"Yes, but I'll never leave here," said Erwin, and a faint smile flickered on his lips.

C H A P T E R

24

Agents and speculators continued to descend upon the house. They would come in the evening, measure the floors, poke everywhere, to prove to Karl that the house was old and small. Sometimes they would interrupt the negotiations to speak warmly about the past. Many of them had known Karl's parents, their shop in the center, and his infamous Aunt Franzi. Karl knew this was merely a ruse. In business, everything is allowed. Finally, unable to restrain himself, he scolded them: "If you want to buy, you're welcome, but I won't permit this idle poking about." They were amazed by his outspokenness, and one of them said, "We're not looking for bargains, but we can't take risks now."

"You'll have to decide."

"If we're not wanted here, we'll go."

"You can look around, but without poking."

"What do you mean by 'poking'? What's this 'poking'?" one of the merchants asked him.

"I am referring to certain rude gestures."

"Excuse me, Karl," a merchant addressed him directly. "You're talking to us as if we were creatures you'd never seen before. We're the same old Jews you've known all your life. True, we didn't study in gymnasium, but you don't have to treat us like criminals."

"I didn't call you criminals."

"Then what's the problem?"

"It's certain gestures."

"Ah, well . . . ," said the merchants, "then Jews aren't welcome here. No matter. The others don't like us either. Not even our children. Fine. Good night."

Karl regretted that he had failed to express himself properly. The merchants, despite everything, were still human beings, and usually he was careful, but this time his emotions got the better of his good sense and he had overdone it.

One of the Jews who came to see the house, a short man with an austere expression, voiced a strange wish. He said, "If God guides my steps, I will buy this house and make it into a synagogue for travelers. The Jews are dwindling, but a few will always remain." Karl wanted to tell him that his reasons were irrelevant to the sale, but the man's ascetic face gave him pause. The man went on to speak about the urgent need to establish small, pleasant synagogues for travelers. There have been many conversions, and even simple Jews were vulnerable. Havens were needed for times of trouble.

"To whom are you making this argument?" Karl interrupted.

"To myself, only to myself. This house pleases me. Its ceiling is old-fashioned, but a low ceiling is good for a synagogue, and pleasant trees grow in the courtyard. A synagogue should be surrounded by trees. Trees bring tranquility into the heart. We need that. I am so frightened by how our numbers have dwindled."

"And that is why you wish to buy the house?" Karl asked, getting back to business.

"I would very much like to. If God brings me prosperity, I will sell my house and buy this one. This house would make a marvelous synagogue. We have a Torah scroll at home, and also a bookcase. Whoever wishes to come, may a blessing be upon him."

"Where are you from, sir?" Karl changed his tone.

"From Eisenberg, about seventy kilometers from here. Many Jews lived there once. Now only my wife and me. All of them converted. It's difficult to live among converts. They stare at you all the time. I never did anyone harm."

"There aren't many Jews here either."

"I know, sir, I know, but there will always be travelers

here. This is a crossroads, and at crossroads there are always Jews. We must help the few, they are deserving of our assistance."

"We're leaving this place," said Karl.

"Where does a Jew go these days?" asked the man.

"To the provinces."

"You're right: in the provinces there is still Jewish life. I too would leave everything and go there, but my wife is very ill, and my two sons have converted and moved away from us. It's hard to bear that shame."

"Where do your sons live?" Karl asked, cautiously.

"Not far from here, in the Warburg Estates. At first we would see them, but in recent years, they have drawn away from us. They were wrong. I wouldn't change my faith for anything in the world."

"Why not?" Karl asked provocatively.

"Because I'm a Jew. There's no advantage in it, but that's what I am. No less and no more. You understand me, don't you?" There was a sudden silence. The man's face expressed a kind of satisfaction for successfully stating his opinion. Then he raised his head and said, "This house is very fine. We'll make it into a fine synagogue. My wife and I need very little, one room. If we manage to assemble a *minyan* on *shabbes*, that will be our reward. You understand me, don't you?"

"I shouldn't conceal from you the fact that I, too, have converted," Karl said with startling coolness.

"Pardon me, I beg your pardon. But I sincerely thought you were a Jew. I was mistaken—I'm always mistaken. Forgive me if I've insulted you. It was unintentional," he said, retreating toward the door.

"I'll gladly sell you the house," Karl said, attempting to reassure him.

"With God's help I'll be back. My house is quite large. And I'll add some of my savings, if necessary, to buy this house. It will make a beautiful synagogue. You're not angry with me, I hope."

"No. Why?"

After a moment he said, "It's hard to sell houses in Eisenberg. Before, business flourished there. Now everything sits idle. Maybe that's the way it should be. Who knows? Everything has changed so quickly. I don't understand a thing."

"Don't be discouraged," said Karl.

"You're right, you're right in every respect," said the man, smiling strangely.

Later, Gloria, who had witnessed the negotiations, said, "It's been a long time since I've seen a face like that."

"What do you mean?"

"His face—it was full of wonder."

In the end, Karl sold the house to one of the city tanners, a tall, coarse man who had made an unpleasant comment the moment he entered the house. The tanner offered a sum not much more than that offered by the merchants, but for some reason Karl accepted his offer on the spot, without bargaining.

When the transaction was concluded, Gloria burst into tears. Karl hugged her and said, "There's no reason to be afraid. Everything here is rotten to the core. The provinces are quiet and pleasant, and we'll live there without people lying in wait for us—without enemies."

"And we'll leave all this behind?"

"We'll be free, and that's more important than property."

"I'm frightened. Why am I so frightened?"

Thus ended his life in Neufeld. He thought of touring the city to say goodbye to the spots he loved, but now that seemed unnecessarily painful. As always, Gloria did what she felt needed to be done. She put on a scarf and went to say farewell to his parents' graves. Since the attack, her forehead expressed a new seriousness. Karl understood: she was more closely bound to this house than he. She had been a part of his parents' lives, and his grandparents', and if there was anyone who had been shaped by them, it was Gloria and not he. More than once he had thought of that, but this time he knew it was true, and it pained him.

Gloria returned from the cemetery and immediately began to pack. She laid out each garment carefully, as if it was something she had just bought. He almost said to her, "Why are you taking these things? They're worn-out." But when he saw her determination, he was silent. Thus, his clothes from the gymnasium and his parents' clothes were packed up together with the ones he still wore.

Toward evening he thought of visiting Hochhut. At the door to the ward he told Dr. Meisler that he wanted to say farewell to Hochhut as he was leaving the city the next day. Though Hochhut had not been his friend, Karl felt that he had atoned for his deeds by his suffering.

"Why do you want to see him? He's not Hochhut anymore." The doctor concealed nothing.

"I just want a word."

On the ground floor, on his knees and wearing a dirty nightshirt, was a creature that, from a distance, resembled a boy. But for a few distinctive features, Karl would not have recognized him.

"Hello there, Hochhut," Karl addressed him. At this the little creature shrank as if he were going to sink into the earth.

"It's Karl Hübner, don't you remember me?" There was no response.

"Don't you remember Mr. Hübner?" the doctor said.

"What does he want?" came the words from the creature's mouth.

"He's come to visit you."

"I don't like it when people come to visit me." Now Karl identified the familiar sound of his voice, the emphatic "I" that Hochhut, in his greatness, used to employ at every opportunity.

"I'm going away soon. I came to say goodbye."

"Have a safe trip, my friend." Karl noted the phrase "my friend," an expression Hochhut always reserved for people beneath him.

"How do you feel?"

"Excellent," said the creature, smiling.

Karl wanted to say something more, but seeing Hochhut's hands tremble, he changed his mind. Meisler walked him to the door and asked, "Where are you going?"

"To the provinces."

"What will someone like you do there?"

"He'll relax," said Karl jokingly.

From there he headed straight for Kirzl's bar. He planned to have a drink and then go back to the rabbi's house to throw out the squatters. The bar was nearly empty, and Kirzl sat with him, telling him her troubles, and those of the people around her. Karl told her that he was going to leave the city the next day.

"And is Gloria going with you?"

"Yes."

Upon hearing Karl's answer, a wicked smile flickered in her eyes. It was clear that this woman too had known sin and enjoyed it. "May Jesus watch over you." she said, the smile disappearing from her eyes. Karl, who had intended to take his leave of her with a kiss, merely said goodbye and departed.

Gloria didn't shut her eyes all that night. She continued to pack, shoving things in and tying up her bundles. Karl knew not to interfere. The next day, when the carriage driver and his two sturdy sons arrived and began loading the suitcases and crates, Gloria said to them, "Be careful, people, be careful." She immediately began to wring her hands, the way Aunt Betty had done.

Freddy was waiting for them at the railway platform.

In his winter coat he looked wretched and pitiful. "Where are you going?" He couldn't hold back his tears. Karl embraced him and spoke to him as if to a younger brother, "The provinces are not a wilderness. There's life there too. Let everyone do what he can." Stifling his tears, Freddy helped load the suitcases and crates. He stood on the platform until the train disappeared from view.

C H A P T E R

25

Karl bought tickets for Cracow. Once the train got under way, the conductor traced their route on the map, and to Karl's surprise he found Rosow. "Gloria," he called out in excitement. "It isn't every day that a man passes by his mother's native village. What's the hurry? Let's get off and see it." Gloria was slow to respond. She was still immersed in the abandoned house, still mourning all that she had left behind. She didn't quite grasp what was happening around her.

Karl poured a drink, and the darkness that had clung to him for so many months abruptly abandoned him. He was glad to be leaving Neufeld. As in his distant youth, he felt that his life was advancing into a new phase.

"Gloria," he called out. "We've left the prison."

They were traveling second class, a mixed throng of Jews and gentiles. Fortunately, they had found two seats together and could ignore the others. Gloria was stunned. The swiftness of the last days had frightened her, and she cried and blamed herself. Karl assured her again that there was nothing to worry about. Life in the provinces was quiet, and after resting they would set out on extended journeys, like those he and Martin had made during their summer vacations.

Had it not been for a tiny incident, fatigue would have overcome them and they would have fallen asleep. But as it happened, one of the Jews, a man in his sixties, not unsympathetic looking, approached Karl and asked where he was going. The question was completely ordinary, the kind one Jew casually asks another. But Karl was annoyed. "That's *my* business," he snapped.

"I meant no harm." The Jew was stunned.

"I don't care to answer your question," said Karl.

"You're a strange one," said the Jew, who went sadly on his way.

After a day and a half, the train finally stopped in Rosow. Together Karl and Gloria took their suitcases and crates and descended to the platform. Peasants in Ruthenian costume dragged sacks of grain to the freight car. Other peasants rushed to take seats in the third-class car.

The station was small and made of wood, and now, after the long winter, the beams were covered with moss and mildew.

"I don't understand a word I hear," said Karl gaily, as if he had reached an unknown land.

"And I understand every word," chuckled Gloria.

Karl was moved by the light, the tall trees, and the crisp air. The peasants who had come on the train loaded the wares they had bought in the city onto wagons that had come for them and then began the climb up the mountain. The station soon emptied.

"Where is the stationmaster?" Karl wondered.

"We'll find him," said Gloria, like someone who has returned to a familiar place.

Soon a tall peasant arrived wearing a red cap. He turned out to be the stationmaster. Gloria asked him about the place, and he answered her in a tumult of words. Unlike the railway clerks in Neufeld, his uniform was sloppy and smelled of manure. Evidently he had just come in from the fields and would soon return to them. His job in the station was only part-time.

"What did he say?" Karl asked after the man went away.

"He said we'd do better to ask the Jews. They know everything."

"The Jews, the Jews," Karl hummed. Then he added, "I would like to rest on one of these hills for a while." Gloria spread a cloth on the ground and prepared cheese and egg sandwiches. Karl noticed: when she had spoken with the stationmaster, her face had changed and she resembled the peasant women who had just left the station.

"How long has it been since you last spoke Ruthenian?"

"Since I left my parents' house."

"And you understand every word?"

"It's my mother tongue. You don't forget that."

Later, for some reason, he asked, "Is Ruthenian a hard language?"

"The people who speak it understand it very well," she teased.

Karl smiled. He hadn't expected an answer like that.

Meanwhile, a wagon entered the station courtyard. Gloria greeted the driver and asked if there were any vacant houses. The peasant pointed to a solitary house on the hilltop across the way. Karl shouted, "That's it!"

"We'll go up and see it," said Gloria, and together they loaded their belongings.

"Where do the Jews live?" she asked.

"Down below," said the peasant, chuckling as if he had been asked about something embarrassing.

"Is there a grocery store there?"

"The Jews have everything."

Spring blew everywhere. In his gymnasium days, he had spoken a lot about living close to nature. The history teacher used to call Rousseau "the prophet of the new era." Back then he and Martin had both dreamt about a house in the mountains, of tending orchards, and of life without Jews and without bureaucracy. But the dream hadn't lasted long. After finishing gymnasium, Martin went to law school and Karl began his career in the municipal government. They would often recall their dreams and laugh. After divorcing his first wife, Martin wanted to buy a country house, but he sank deeper and deeper into his work, and the dream was forgotten.

After half an hour of slow travel, they reached the hilltop. The house was a large peasant dwelling, three rooms in the front and three behind. Next to the house was a barn—with no animals—and a woodshed. Until a year ago the old man had kept the farm going, but since his wife's death he could no longer manage. He was ninety-three and he wanted to live with his daughter. If he became ill, she would care for him.

"And how much is it?"

Gloria conducted the bargaining well, and finally, after numerous refusals and agreements, a deal was made.

"That chapter is over," said the old man as he parted from them.

"We'll take good care of the house," Gloria promised.

"May God keep you, you're young."

"May He keep you, too."

"To my regret, I'm on my way to Him," the old man joked.

It wasn't so much a house as a kingdom. In the yard there were apple, pear, and cherry trees. The cherries were already ripe. To the right of the orchard was nestled a well-tended vegetable garden, and beyond it lay the most beautiful beds of flowers.

"I told you!" he burst out in joy.

Gloria was more restrained. The abundance frightened her. It reminded her of her forgotten house in the village. Before long they were standing by the stove making coffee. Gloria, it turned out, had brought many supplies, including coffee, tea, and spices. Of course they lacked dairy products, not to mention herring, which Karl loved.

"Where are the Jews? Where are they?" Karl asked in a bemused voice.

"They're down below. We'll go to them tomorrow."

Their kingdom was bigger than at first they realized. There was a toolshed, two greenhouses where the old man grew strawberries and a special variety of tomatoes, a little grove of trees, and a field of sunflowers and corn.

"I'm overwhelmed," said Karl.

"Me too."

"I'm going to pick you up and declare you the queen of Rosow."

"Don't pick me up so high."

The night fell without their noticing it, and they were drunk with the scents and colors. Neufeld suddenly seemed far away, almost nonexistent.

"I've forgotten everything," he said.

"That's just how it seems."

"I swear to you."

Words he hadn't used in years floated up. For example, the expression "splendid treasure." Once Aunt Franzi had brought a giant bottle of perfume, and on its label the words "Splendid Treasure" had been written.

"What's happening to me?" he wondered.

"You're tired."

When darkness fell he stripped off her clothes and shouted, "I love you to the high heavens!"

CHAPTER

26

May was at its height, and Gloria worked in the garden, hoeing and watering as needed. Karl would come to keep her company. Her face had darkened to a uniform tan, and she walked barefoot without hesitation. For a moment it seemed to him that things would stay this way. In a day or two the turmoil of the city would fade, and the silence of the trees would fill his soul. The dizziness of the mountain air stripped him of memory after memory. Suddenly, the years that had passed seemed as if they never were.

"What's happening to me?" he kept asking.

"Don't you feel well?"

"Everything seems so far away."

"That's just how it seems."

Somehow they put off the descent into Rosow. Gloria would say, "We must go down for supplies. Soon I won't have anything to cook." But Karl wasn't in a hurry, and he kept postponing the descent from day to day. The place captivated him completely. He would spend hours in the toolshed, in the greenhouse, or in the grove of trees that hid the field of corn and sunflowers. The light intoxicated him. At midday, he would tumble down onto a mat and fall asleep.

At last they had no choice but to go down.

Rosow lay on a small plateau surrounded by green hilltops that made the town look even smaller. When they arrived, they saw a village square surrounded by about twenty small houses. That was Rosow.

"Where are you from?" asked the grocer.

"From Neufeld," Karl told him.

It turned out that the people there were observant but not fanatically religious. In the little bookstore religious books in dark covers were displayed alongside used books in German, and next to them were stacks of magazines.

They went from store to store purchasing supplies. The shops were small but crammed with merchandise. Everyone greeted them pleasantly. Some asked questions, others kept silent, but no one bothered them. Later, they sat in the café and ordered coffee and strudel. From the window they could see their house perched on the hilltop.

"It's pretty," said Gloria.

Karl felt dizzy and closed his eyes.

Gloria had many faces that spring. In the morning she worked in the garden, and in the afternoon she scrubbed clothes on the washboard. Karl brought water from the well and hung the clothes up to dry. During her work hours, her face was calm and focused, and in the evening, speech came to her with great effort.

"How do you feel?" he would probe.

"Fine, why do you ask?"

Once he had imagined that isolation would bring a person to speech. It seemed he was mistaken. He, too, had lost the use of words. The mountain increasingly enveloped him in oblivion. It was as if his life had merged with the vegetation, and his memory had vanished. But sometimes it would reappear in a painful burst of brightness. Past visions would return to him and burst into flame—the relatives who used to invade the house when he was a child, filling it with foreign smells. Their joy and weeping and the conversations long into the night. Even then he had known, without understanding the language, that they were discussing painful experiences from which there was no relief except to race from place to place. When he entered the gymnasium, the relatives stopped coming.

He was vulnerable. How vulnerable he was, he himself did not know. Sudden memories would seize him, digging in and terrifying him. The light not only put him to sleep but cruelly illuminated several dark places in his soul. For example, the frequent, and repugnant, visits to

Victoria's. The sour taste that remained in his mouth after each visit. The conversion. For some reason the whole business began to disturb him. Gloria didn't know how to respond. She retained the beliefs and customs she had absorbed in the house, observing the Sabbath and never buying pork. When he asked if she thought he ought to go to church, she said, "You mustn't bend your knee."

"Why not?"

"Because it doesn't suit you."

He laughed, and Gloria felt relieved.

Now he remembered: when Martin and Freddy converted, it was as if they had swum far beyond him, and he had to catch up. The connection with Freddy had been severed, but he would meet Martin from time to time. Indirectly, Martin had urged him to convert. Once he said, "Conversion freed me. For years I felt I was boxed in, in a cage." Indeed, in the first months after his conversion, Karl, too, had felt relief. He thought he was finally on the right course, that he would go forward without delay. Only later did he learn that the church was oppressive if you didn't believe in the Holy Trinity. He kept hearing his mother shouting at him into the wee hours: "If promotion requires you to convert, then convert." When they were sitting *shivah* for her, the house had hummed like a bee-hive. Many people came to comfort him and his father. It seemed to Karl then that many of them had come not only to console but also as a sign of their resistance to Father Merser. One mustn't submit, the mourning faces entreated. Despair is at the root of all sin. During the seven days of the *shivah*, the mourners' faces seemed to have become believing faces once more. We are Jews, and there is nothing to be ashamed of. And at the end of the mourning period, they cried out: The Jewish people lives! These were the wretched merchants of the center, whose sons and daughters had been ensnared by Father Merser's wiles and had left their parents' homes in disgust.

C H A P T E R

27

Finally, he told them his name.

"Karl Hübner." They couldn't believe their eyes.

Then he began going down to Rosow every day. In the little café he found newspaper readers who were well versed in the complex affairs of the Empire, a few money changers, and, of course, chess players. For hours he would sit and play chess. His daily schedule, which so far had been governed by his moods, seemed to settle down. In the morning he still helped Gloria. The afternoon and evening he spent below, in the café, among people who surrounded him with unspoken affection.

"He's Gusta Hübner's son," they kept saying, marveling.

Nothing was unknown to them. They knew that Karl had finished gymnasium with high honors, that his parents couldn't afford to send him to the university, that he had done well in his job and had risen to the level of municipal secretary. Of course, they also knew about his conversion, but they overlooked it. In their eyes he was simply Gusta Hübner's son.

Toward evening Gloria would come and they would do their shopping. From his mother's descriptions, Gloria could identify many of the houses, including the house where his mother had lived. The place was without beauty, and poverty was visible in every corner. But Gloria noticed: the women were dressed neatly, the children played quietly, and in the shops they wrapped the goods in clean paper.

"My mother never told me a thing."

"She told you, but you were very busy."

"That's true."

On their way home they would stop in the tavern to sip a drink or two. The pub was always full at that hour. "Let's buy a bottle and sit quietly at home," Gloria suggested more than once, but Karl was drawn to the place, perhaps because it reminded him of Kirzl's bar. Here, too, the desperate faces stood out.

"There are too many angry people here," Gloria remarked.

"There's nothing to be afraid of. We're not bothering anybody."

It was here, amid the noise, that he told Gloria about some of the anguish he had never mentioned at home, about his complicated relationship with Martin, and the fear that Hochhut had struck in him from the time he had first met him in gymnasium. But these were echoes of past days. Now the house and the surrounding hills filled his soul. In the early morning hours dense light flowed in, and they took a long while to prepare breakfast. The coffee that Gloria made had an inebriating effect that bubbled in him for hours. Afterward, their paths would divurge. Gloria would head for the garden and Karl would go off into the grove of trees, or as far as the cornfield.

Thus the first weeks passed. Then he was more and more drawn to Rosow, especially to the merchants who played chess so well. He was astonished by the amount of knowledge that had accumulated in this remote spot. Here they read not only newspapers but journals, books of popular science, history, and literature.

"How long will you stay with us?"

"As long as possible. I feel good here." He didn't hide his emotions.

What would happen and how did not concern him at all. The days sustained him. At night he would fall upon Gloria full of strength and desire. In sleep, he was closer to her than when awake. The words that had escaped him were suddenly within reach. Like the phrase "with all his might," which he recalled at night. Sometimes he would wake Gloria up, calling out, "I've found the right words."

"What have you found?" she asked nervously.

It was hard to explain to her what joy he felt.

He got into arguments in the tavern. There were a few retired policemen and soldiers who spoke German and tried to prove to him that all the evils in the world came only from the Jews. They had all the money. If not for the Jews, there wouldn't be so many wretched people in the world.

"That's a lie," he shouted.

"It's the truth."

"You should be ashamed of yourself."

"What do I have to be ashamed of?"

"It's forbidden to slander."

"There's no point in arguing," Gloria tried to pull him away, but Karl was resolved: one must not suppress the truth; it must be proclaimed aloud. Those arguments didn't interfere with his happiness. The summer lights enveloped them from morning until late at night. At night they would collapse onto mats together, like children after a day of swimming in the river.

CHAPTER

28

The summer was still at its height: the sky was broad and open, Gloria was on her knees, picking vegetables in the garden, while Karl lay dozing at the foot of a birch tree. While everything was bright and clear, not a cloud in a perfect sky, a wagon hitched to two strong horses wheeled into the courtyard. A man dressed in a long raincoat and boots stepped down from it slowly, deliberately, like a man who had come to avenge an insult.

"Karl," the man called out.

"I'm over here," said Karl, sounding trapped.

It was Freddy.

"What are you doing here?" asked Karl, as if in a dream.

"I was worried about you," answered Freddy, a little short of breath.

"There's nothing to worry about. We have a roomy house," said Karl, embracing him.

"I'm upset about your leaving."

"Everything is fine. Here's Gloria."

Gloria rose and approached, an embarrassed blush glowing in her tanned face. Then for a moment she froze, as if caught in a hiding place. Freddy lowered his head, realizing he was intruding.

Later, they sat at the table and Gloria prepared coffee and sandwiches. Freddy looked more and more uncomfortable, with both his innocence and clumsiness blossoming anew. Karl tried to console him, but didn't yet know how. He was sorry Freddy had dragged himself such a long distance.

"How long have you been on the road?"

"For two days. I'm used to travel. People are always calling for me, but this time I myself chose the way," he said, his guileless smile standing out more than ever.

"Whom do you see in the city?" Karl tried to draw him out.

"Nobody, just patients."

"I help Gloria. We have a garden," Karl said. Something of Freddy's awkwardness clung to him.

"And this is how you see your future?" Freddy, never far from a cliché.

"What do you mean—'my future'?"

"How else should I put it?"

"I feel good here."

"And you don't miss people?"

"Life is simple here. The mountain accepts you as you are. And it costs very little."

Freddy was astonished, as if he realized it wasn't a matter of madness but of will.

"If you feel good here, I suppose I have nothing to say."

"I feel excellent. These peaks are marvelous. I don't need anything more."

"I guess I was wrong," said Freddy, narrowing his shoulders.

Gloria once again assumed the demeanor of a housemaid, of one who doesn't sit at the table but who serves and immediately withdraws into her corner.

"There is everything a person needs here. I wasn't happy in Neufeld."

"You won't return to us?"

"No. I've resigned."

"I miss you," said Freddy, smiling foolishly.

"I'm not going back to Neufeld."

"Father Merser asked after you."

"I wasn't very happy with him during the past year. He's grown arrogant. Why did he baptize Elsa Ring? You don't baptize an eighty-year-old person. Someone that age should die in his own bed and be gathered unto his ancestors in peace. At that age you don't confuse people's minds. Do you understand me?"

"Could I have a drink?" Freddy lifted his head.

"Let's go down to the village. We can have one there."

When Freddy got up, Karl saw how he had aged. His bright face, which had been kneaded by his good-heartedness and concern for the community, had gotten very fat, his eye sockets had turned black, and his posture had become bent. It made Karl angry that peasants called for him night after night, because they were too lazy to go to his clinic. What thankless work. Devoted people like Freddy should have good wives, merciful wives, wives devoted in heart and soul—not grasping, selfish wives, he wanted to cry out. He hastily put on his jacket and said, "Gloria, I'm going down. I'm going to show Freddy Rosow. Should I bring something for you?"

"We have everything we need."

The tavern was overflowing. Peasant men and women crowded around the bar, the air was thick with the smell of vodka, and a wall of tobacco smoke blunted one's vision. Karl pushed his way through and returned immediately with two glasses of cognac.

"I need a drink," Freddy confessed.

"I do too. But, you know, here sometimes you can sink into yourself without it. You should watch your health, Freddy."

"I do. I'm absolutely fine," he mumbled.

"I wouldn't get up in the middle of the night anymore. They should come to the clinic."

"What can I do? I'm a doctor."

"You're a doctor, not a priest."

"I take good care of myself. I have a warm sheepskin coat for traveling at night, and it protects me."

The warmth of their youth seemed to return as they sat and sipped. Karl promised Freddy that this wasn't his last stop, that he still had it in mind to do things. Perhaps one day he would come and visit him.

It was sunset, and the tavern was crammed with people. "Why don't we go out for a stroll," Karl suggested. But Freddy preferred the noise. After a few drinks he forgot his reason for coming and spoke about the plans he had never realized: the clinics he would open to the general public, and the assistance he would offer the needy. At first he thought he could gain the support of the owners of the estates and mines for his plan. They had insisted on seeing written memoranda, so he wrote out very detailed proposals. In the end, they didn't even reply. Now he would turn to the Ministry of Health.

Don't do that, my dear fellow, Karl wanted to say. I know them very well. No good will come from them. But seeing his hurt face, he refrained.

As they drank, Freddy spoke about Martin and his blood pressure, his frequent trips to Winterhof, how much he drank, the women who had driven him crazy, and his impudent clients. Finally, he blamed himself for not sending him to get a second opinion.

"You should know that he had contempt for you as a doctor."

"That doesn't change a thing. A physician can't pay

attention to insults. A physician has to be able to endure that sort of thing."

"But we expect a certain loyalty from friends," said Karl, unwilling to give in.

"A physician must overcome that, too."

Karl was astonished. He had never seen such submissiveness, as though Freddy had taxed himself all these years in order to reach this level. Nor could he stop now. He would wander from village to village, and patient to patient, until he wore out his soul.

"Why won't you use your clinic in the city?"

"My patients are scattered among the villages."

"You should make them come to you."

"No, they're all infected with typhus."

"Isn't there a danger of your becoming infected?"

"The physician is immune," said Freddy, and a mischievous smile brightened his eyes.

Later, silence fell upon them. Darkness clung to the windows, and the peasants were already drunk. They cursed the owner of the bar and his wife, and the tax officials who had come by train the day before to confiscate property and to arrest people.

"It's late, where's the train?" Freddy awoke.

"Why don't you stay with us for a few days?"

"I can't. A typhus epidemic is raging."

"Too bad."

"I brought you some money."

"No, my dear fellow. I got severance pay from the

municipality. Don't forget, I worked there for seventeen years."

"But you don't have a regular salary."

"I received a lot of money. You have nothing to worry about."

Even on the way to the train, half drunk and leaning on Karl's arm, Freddy kept talking about how Martin had failed to take care of his body, which he called "the temple of the soul." Karl wanted to scold him and say, you're wasting your devotion on people who are unworthy of it. But seeing his misery, he merely said, "Everything will be fine, my dear fellow, everything will be fine," and he pressed him to his heart.

CHAPTER

29

The summer came to an end, and Gloria was preparing vegetable soup, spinach pies, and potato knishes. He could ignore the dark clouds that spread over the mountains and say to himself: that dreary color isn't forever. Soon the snow will come and spread out its canopies, and all the gloom will vanish. He could have said it, but for some reason he didn't. Freddy had left a sadness in his soul that fermented within him. He walked down to the village early, played a game or two of chess, and then went straight to the tavern. A few drinks would calm him down. He would sit and listen to the retired soldiers whose coarse, stale jokes amused him. He would return home in a haze. Gloria wasn't pleased by his coming home late, but she said nothing. In her heart, she knew he needed some release.

He didn't always return relaxed. If people spoke out against the Jews or the Gypsies, he would stand up and protest. "Don't blame the minorities," he argued. "They're human beings too—they too have sleepless nights and aches and pains."

"But they're the children of Satan."

"There are no children of Satan. There are good people and bad people."

Once, when the discussion heated up, one of the soldiers, a war invalid, stood up and called out, "What are you, mister, an Austrian or a Jew?"

"I'm a human being."

Karl knew he was using slogans from his gymnasium days that had no connection to real life, but they burst out of him every time a racial slur was flung into the air of the tavern.

"He's crazy," they declared, dismissing his words.

Autumn showed a clouded face. One day he imagined that sturdy horses, like those that had brought Freddy, were approaching the house with muffled steps. Soon the reins would be released and they would trample the vegetables and flowers. He knew that if he picked up the whip and went outside he could drive them off, but he felt that it was no longer in his power. His limbs were frozen. The horses drew closer, with a single desire—to trample the garden that Gloria had nurtured. Why don't you stop them?" he wanted to shout with all his might. Gloria didn't seem to sense the danger. She was standing by the oven, cooking a spinach pie. Karl knew that it was only an unpleasant daydream, but still, it was hard for him to forgive Gloria her indifference.

"Why are you standing idly by?" A shout finally burst from his throat.

"What's the matter?" asked Gloria.

"Nothing."

"You shouted, or did it just seem that way?"

"It seemed that way."

Still, that autumn his daily schedule remained orderly. Gray clouds continued to surround the house, but there were also hours as clear as crystal. He helped Gloria in the garden and brought baskets full of vegetables inside. The feel of the loose soil and the moist vegetables made him so happy that tears came to his eyes. But he spent more hours in the café, playing chess and arguing. The Jewish merchants liked him but did not agree with his views.

"You mustn't bribe the police. Bribery corrupts."

"If we don't pay off the police, we'll be fair game for anyone."

"You mustn't be afraid."

"It's not fear, it's the choice between life and death."

It made him angry that healthy men, dependable and devoted to the community, should flinch every time anyone mentioned the police. A person must defend his honor.

"What should they do?" asked Gloria.

"Learn to defend themselves."

"Jews don't know how to use weapons."

"It's time they learned."

A strange anger simmered within him. Gloria wanted to accompany him to the café, but he preferred to go alone. Every day he would go down, and every day he would carry the arguments from the café to the tavern. In the evening, when he returned home, his face was weary, his eyes angered, and a kind of restlessness vibrated in his fingers.

"Karl, what should I cook for you?"

"Vegetable soup."

She would cook everything that grew in the garden to cheer him up, but Karl wasn't as happy as before. Distant matters returned to haunt him. Once, out of the blue, he said, "I'm not sorry I converted. It freed me from a deep pit. Now that I'm up on the surface, I can at least see and hear. It's not much, but it's something." Gloria didn't understand what he was talking about. It pained her that he was no longer meticulous in his dress. Every day she ironed a shirt and a pair of trousers for him, but when he returned at night, his clothes were rumpled and stained.

I mustn't criticize him, she told herself.

On Rosh Hashanah she spread a white cloth on the table and put down saucers of honey and apple slices.

"What's this?" asked Karl, without raising his head.

"It's the eve of Rosh Hashanah."

"Where do you find such optimism?" he said, and a thin laugh twisted his lips.

Melancholy didn't overcome him every evening. Sometimes his face brightened. He would sit on the mat with Gloria and they would have their drinks with salty crackers. His memory was clear and his movements spry. He would imitate the municipal clerks and bring her to tears with laughter.

The next day she would plead with him, "Don't go down."

"I must," he would say and walk off.

CHAPTER

30

On Yom Kippur he went down and, to his surprise, found the square deserted. The stores were shuttered, and only a few horses were tethered outside. A cold wind blew between the naked trees. From the tiny synagogue, lit by candles, came a low hum. Had he entered, they would have been glad to see him. As he stood there, he remembered his mother, as he hadn't for many days: young, her face full of life. He was pressed to her breast and wrapped in her arms. A customer had tried to amuse him, but he had been afraid of him. Shrinking, he gripped his mother and curled up in her big wool sweater. The

sweet fragrance of wool mixed with the scent of soap surrounded him with intoxicating pleasure.

From where he stood he could see the house on the
hill. The day before, Gloria had prepared the dining room
with care, reminding him of Yom Kippur at home. Again,
he said to himself: Gloria remembers more than I do. Life
in our house had penetrated into her, yet it left no impres-
sion on me. Gloria, he wanted to ask, are you religious?
Do you understand the meaning of what you're doing, or
is it just habit? But he changed his mind. Gloria's acts
were so modest, and the words he thought to utter were
so pompous and vulgar. After she had tidied up the
kitchen, she spread a white cloth over the table.

But he could not restrain his tongue. "Do you believe
in God?" asked Karl.

This time she wasn't flustered and answered, "I
believe in God."

"In the God of the Jews?"

"I left my house when I was very young because
things were very bad. Your father and mother gave me
shelter, clothing, and bread to eat. I love the Jewish holidays because they're quiet."

"You didn't answer my question, Gloria."

"What was your question?"

"It doesn't matter," he said, laughing.

Later, they sat in silence. Karl didn't smoke or drink,
and he fell asleep very early. He slept all morning. In the
afternoon, he got up and dressed and immediately hurried

down to town. On the way he felt a threat in the air, but he dismissed the feeling and continued. He wanted to reach Rosow in time to see the people walking to synagogue. He had forgotten that at this hour, close to the concluding service, not even little children go out. When he reached Rosow he saw with his own eyes: no one. A cold emptiness blew in every corner.

While standing in the empty square, he noticed two young peasants near the tavern throwing stones. First it seemed they were throwing at a target. But when Karl drew close he saw that they were aiming at windows.

"Why are you breaking windows?" he asked as he approached them.

"The Jews closed the tavern and there's nothing to drink."

"You should know," Karl addressed them quietly, "that this is a very sacred holiday for them."

"To hell with their holidays. People have to drink."

"It's a holiday of spiritual accounting," said Karl, strangely.

"What's he talking about?" the young peasant asked his friend, who was shorter.

"About having respect," answered Karl.

"We shit on your respect."

"I suggest you not use foul language."

"I piss on this place."

"Young man, that's indecent language."

"I piss on you."

Now he had no choice but to do what he always did

when confronted with bullies. He grappled with the first and then with the second, shaking them and throwing them to the ground. They were thunderstruck, their legs waved in the air, and they begged for mercy.

"You're not getting away from here until you apologize to the Jews."

"We apologize," they mumbled together.

"Not like that. I want to hear you ask forgiveness of the Jews of Rosow for desecrating their holiday."

They repeated what he said, word for word. In the end, he let them go and they ran for their lives.

When he returned home, it was already night. Gloria was sitting at the table and waiting for him. The holy day was inside her. Her face was pale from the fast and a weak light glowed in her eyes.

"A blessed year, Karl," she said, coming toward him. Later, he told her about the incident in the square. Gloria listened and said nothing. In her heart, she knew that the peasants wouldn't easily forgive an insult like that. She prepared a full meal and they sat and ate. She wanted to tell Karl something about her father, but a fear that had dwelled in her since childhood rose up and choked her. The words never escaped her mouth.

CHAPTER

31

The next day Gloria noticed that the cabbage patch had been torn up. At first she thought it was a theft, but then she realized it was vandalism. Karl gritted his teeth and, without delay, went down to Rosow. The police station was locked. And when he asked where he should go to lodge a complaint, people shrugged. In the café he realized what that meant. One of the merchants, a clever chess player, explained to him: "You see, one hand washes the other. Those who were once policemen are now thieves and murderers, and tomorrow they'll switch back."

"And that's how it's always been?"

"From time immemorial."

"And no one does anything about this?"

"What is there to be done?"

The nights taught him what village life was really like. Tranquility no longer hid behind its beauty. Wicked hands reached out of the darkness to uproot the garden. Karl no longer slept well. He went out to walk around the house and returned with a stormy look, his mouth clenched in anger.

He went from store to store, trying to buy a pistol. Panicked, the merchants urged him not to do it. Karl was furious. He rejected as so much hot air the argument that the peasants were people of the soil and you had to make allowances for their behavior. If a person defends his honor, he told them, no harm will befall him. In the end, seeing no alternative, he bought a pistol. It was broken and old, but he was sure he could repair it. For a full day he and the jeweler labored, without success, to replace the trigger. But Karl didn't despair. He promised a large sum to anyone who got a working pistol for him. Meanwhile, the merchants avoided him, and he would spend hours in the tavern, drinking and quarreling with the peasants. When he returned home, he immediately announced that he intended to fight. Gloria knew that their lives were now in God's hands and that she could no longer hope to influence Karl.

Nevertheless, she told him, "We must leave this place."

"Not now."

"They're planning to attack us. I know them only too well, I am sad to say."

"We won't sit with our arms folded, either."

The next day the old landlord came and got right to the point. "The villagers are furious. The boys are threatening to set the house on fire. The others are also angry. You mustn't provoke these people. You'd better clear out—for your own safety."

"Tell him we have harmed no one."

"The old man understands that," Gloria said.

"What does he want, then?"

"For us to leave."

"We have harmed no one."

"Stubbornness is the mother of all sin," said the old man, leaving the house.

The siege around the house grew ever tighter. Night after night, horsemen rode into the courtyard, filling it with screams and curses. Karl would go out and shout at them, "Wicked people! We won't give in to your wickedness!" The horsemen responded with contempt. Karl ignored the danger. The desire to stand up to them, face to face, ruled him. Finally one of them stabbed him. Gloria dragged him inside, while stones and curses were hurled at her from all sides. The wound was deep and Gloria bandaged it with a towel.

"We have to get a doctor. How can I get a doctor?" She wrung her hands at the sight of so much blood.

"No need, it will stop." And, indeed, toward morning

the bleeding stopped. And although the pain continued, Karl was in an exalted mood and spoke enthusiastically about Cracow, about the university and the public libraries there. Gloria didn't understand most of what he was saying, but she was pleased that his spirits were high. Once he even mentioned Victoria's, and both of them laughed.

One night he revealed his intentions to her: "We must marry soon."

"What things you think of."

"I decided some time ago."

"You have to get out of here and build a future for yourself. This isn't a good place."

"Don't you love me anymore?"

"I'm not a young woman, and I can't bear you any children." She removed a weight from her mind.

"Don't be silly." He dismissed her words. "As soon as I get better, we'll go to Cracow. It's a pleasant and cultured city. We'll rent a house with big windows. The money we have will last for two years. After that I'll find work. I agree with you: this isn't the right place."

The following days were rainy and dark. One could hear the strong winds and the rushing streams. Gloria brought vegetables and fruit up from the cellar, everything they had stored during the summer. "Now I'll cook us some royal delicacies," she said.

Memories of past days arose as if by a will of their own. The meetings on Tuesdays at Father Merser's house, his sister Clara, and the music.

"How I was tempted to go there I'll never understand. Did you ever meet Father Merser?"

"Never."

"He's truly a magician."

Several times Freddy's name came up. Karl spoke of him now with fondness and longing, as if he were a brother living in exile. The peasants wearing that sweet fellow down every night. That couldn't continue. If there was any reason to return to Neufeld, it was to rescue Freddy from their hands.

The wound hurt a lot, but he was optimistic, promising Gloria he would never quit his struggle. "Life without concern for the community is petty and worthless." Gloria was pleased with every word he said. "We are few, Gloria," he called out one night, "but we are not afraid. The monster is not as powerful as it pretends to be."

The lull turned out to be a brief one. The horsemen returned to the courtyard and threw everything they had at the place, breaking all the windows. After that, they heaped beams and branches onto the front of the house. Now the rooms were dark. Gloria moved Karl to an inner room, where she lit a kerosene lantern and covered him with sheepskin rugs.

"I was mistaken," he murmured.

"What are you talking about?"

"We should have gone directly to Cracow."

"We'll do it. It's not too late."

Karl didn't complain about the pain in his arm, only

about his legs, which were cold. Hot water bottles no longer warmed them. His wound changed color, to a purplish red. Karl now spoke a great deal, and eloquently. The thought that Cracow had a university and public libraries inflamed his imagination. Suddenly he could not forgive his parents. "Other parents took out loans and sent their sons to Vienna," he raged one night. But his anger was mostly directed at Father Merser, for his zeal in converting old women from the nursing home.

Afterward, he spoke only about his cold legs. Gloria rubbed them with her hands. In the end, she stood at the window and called out, "Take the branches away from the entrance to the house! There's no air in here, there's no light!"

"What?" a muffled voice was heard to say.

"Don't you understand? There's a sick man here."

The cold was very painful. Gloria placed three bottles of boiling water at his feet, but even that didn't help. Now he scolded her as if she were his maidservant and ordered her about. She obeyed, saying nothing. From day to day the cold grew more severe. At last he stopped complaining, and his face relaxed. In vain Gloria tried to seal the windows, but the wind blew in with great force. Now the cold gripped her legs as well. She felt its power on her flesh. From time to time Karl would wake up and ask, "What's that noise?"

"It's nothing, my dear."

Thus passed a few more days. Gradually, Gloria was

gripped in the paralyzing web of cold. First she wanted to lie on the couch so as not to disturb him, but at last she climbed into bed and curled up at his side.

That night the peasants poured kerosene on the branches. Within seconds the fire seized the corners of the house and it burst into flames.

ABOUT THE AUTHOR

Aharon Appelfeld was born in 1932 in Czernowitz, Bukovina (now part of Ukraine). At the age of nine, he was imprisoned in a Nazi concentration camp, from which he escaped. Having lost his mother to the Nazis, and separated from his father, he hid in the forests and eventually joined the Soviet army as a kitchen boy, immigrating to Palestine in 1946. The author of twelve internationally acclaimed novels, including *Badenheim 1939*, *The Iron Tracks*, *Unto the Soul*, *The Retreat*, and *The Age of Wonders*, he lives in Jerusalem.